Also by Lorri Horn

Dewey Fairchild, Parent Problem Solver

Dewey Fairchild, Teacher Problem Solver

DEWEY FAIRCHILD,

SIBLING PROBLEM SOLVER

Lorri Horn

Amberjack Publishing
Idaho

AMBERJACK
PUBLISHING

8/19

Amberjack Publishing
1472 E. Iron Eagle Drive
Eagle, ID 83616
amberjackpublishing.com

This book is a work of fiction. Any references to real places are used fictitiously. Names, characters, fictitious places, and events are the products of the author's imagination, and any resemblance to actual persons, living or dead, places, or events is purely coincidental.

10 9 8 7 6 5 4 3 2 1

Hardcover ISBN: 978-1-948705-41-7

eBook ISBN: 978-1-948705-42-4

Library of Congress Cataloging-in-Publication Data
Names: Horn, Lorri, author.
Title: Dewey Fairchild, sibling problem solver / Lorri Horn.
Description: Eagle, ID : Amberjack Publishing, 2019. | Series: Dewey Fairchild ; 3 | Summary: "Dewey Fairchild's problem-solving skills are legendary, but when he expands his business to include sibling problems, he finds himself seeing his oddest clients to date and hatching the craziest of schemes to help siblings get along"-- Provided by publisher.
Identifiers: LCCN 2019013172 (print) | LCCN 2019016816 (ebook) | ISBN 9781948705424 (ebook) | ISBN 9781948705417 (hardback)
Subjects: | CYAC: Middle schools--Fiction. | Schools--Fiction. | Brothers and sisters--Fiction. | Humorous stories. | BISAC: JUVENILE FICTION / Mysteries & Detective Stories. | JUVENILE FICTION / School & Education.
Classification: LCC PZ7.1.H664 (ebook) | LCC PZ7.1.H664 Des 2019 (print) | DDC [Fic]--dc23
LC record available at https://lccn.loc.gov/2019013172

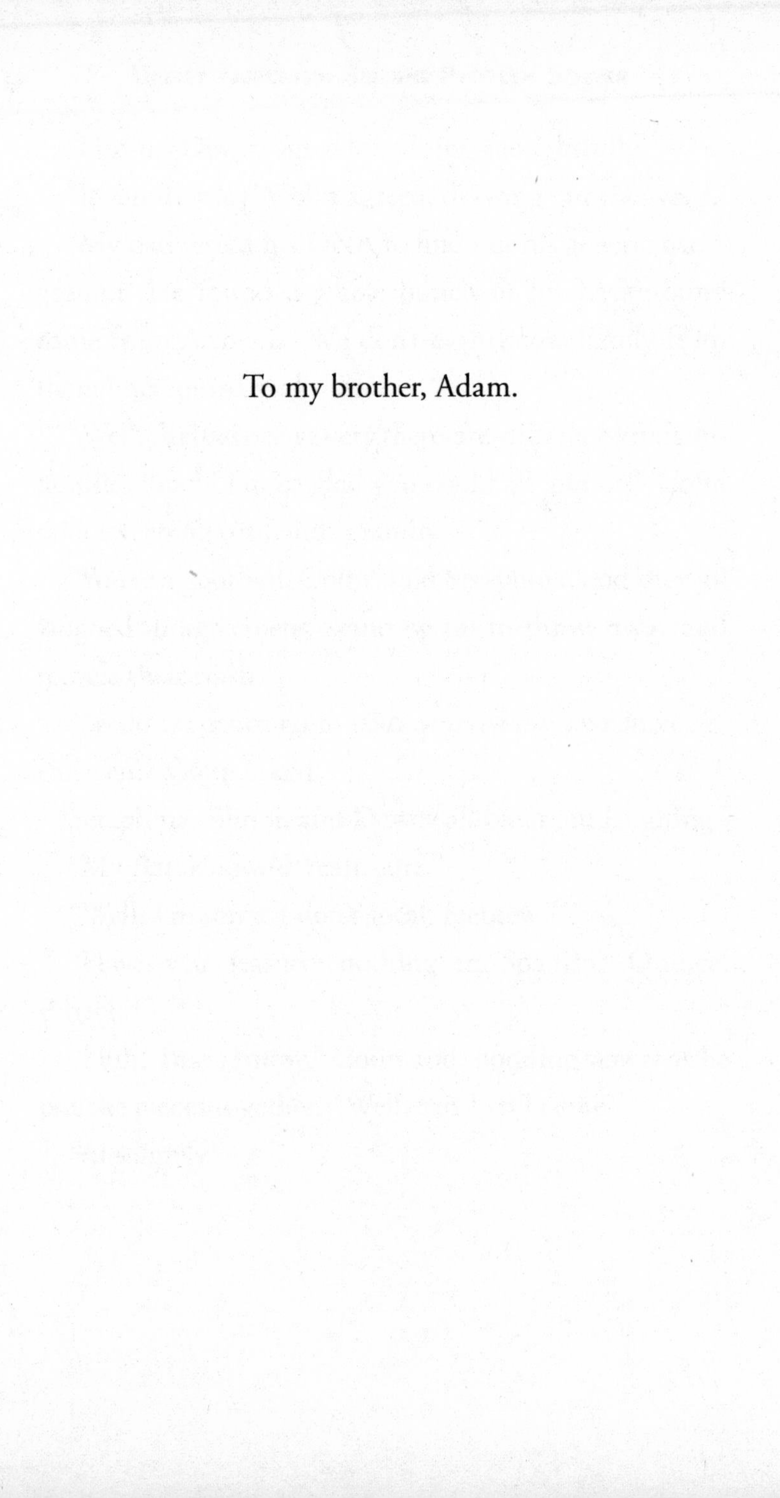

To my brother, Adam.

A New Start

Winter break had been gloriously filled with late nights playing video games and late mornings sleeping in. Now, back at school almost a month later, it was as if those days had never happened at all.

"Good morning, Dewbert! Time to wake up!" his mother chirped as she opened his curtains to the darkness outside.

Dewey moaned. Although each morning waking in the dark was its own form of unique torture, only a few hours at school and he was right back into the swing of the familiar rest of it—classes, vending machines, his friends. Everything had returned to normal, except Clara was still gone. At first, Dewey enjoyed the slower pace that came with the office being closed. It had been a busy end to the fall semester, and he enjoyed carefree afternoons flying his drone and playing computer games when his homework was done.

"What's today, Mom?" he asked, yawning as he stretched.

"Monday."

"No, I mean the date?"

"Oh. The twenty-seventh."

Dewey felt his heart jump into his mouth. He sat up.

"Of January?!"

"Last time I checked," she laughed.

"That's beyond great!"

"Oh, yeah? Why?" she asked, picking up a pair of pants off the floor and folding them. "Are these clean?" She suddenly had second thoughts.

"Yeah. I think so." He didn't answer her question about feeling excited because he couldn't think of a good reason to give her.

Dewey's mom gave him a funny look.

"What'd you do, put a chocolate bar in your pants?"

"I think that's a distinct possibility," Dewey grinned.

"Ugh, Dewey." She threw the pants over her shoulder. "Okay, get up. Make your bed, would you?"

She left to go rouse Dewey's little sister, Emma, who they all called Pooh Bear.

The twenty-seventh meant Clara and Wolfie would finally be back in the office. He threw the sheets and comforter over his pillow. Good enough, he thought. Dewey could hardly wait for his school day to start so that it would end.

Skijoring

When Dewey walked into the office after school, the first thing to hit him was the familiar smell of cookies in the oven. In his mind, Dewey knew that he missed Clara and Wolfie, but now he could feel it in his whole body as the sweet warm smell of cookies lifted him up like a magic carpet.

"Clara? Wolfie?"

Wolfie came running out first, followed closely behind by his ninety-four-year-old assistant Clara Cottonwood. Dewey threw his arms around Clara's shoulders as Wolfie jumped up on his leg.

"Hey, Boy!"

"Good to see you, sir," smiled Clara, warmly hugging

him back. "Wolfie. Down." A timer went off in her kitchen, and she ran off to take the batch of cookies out of the oven. Dewey coaxed Wolfie back up.

"So, how was it?" Dewey plopped down at his desk and began to warm up the computer.

"Marvelous! Wolfie wanted to learn to ski, but I'm afraid he's too small. We still had a time of it zooming in the snow and chasing rabbits, right?" she asked, petting Wolfie.

"What?! Dog skiing?"

"Skijoring. Cross-country skiing with a dog! You hook the dog up and they pull you. But he's only eighteen pounds, and they need to be at least thirty-five."

"Still, a barrel of fun. I'd throw a snowball and it would break. He'd go off searching high and low and come up looking like Father Christmas."

"How about you, sir? What have you to report?"

"Oh, not much. Same ol'. Dad has a new class of kids, and it's his last semester student teaching. Everything else, thankfully, is pretty much the same. I'm wondering how backlogged we are," said Dewey, looking at the chats and texts.

Clara and Dewey had been in business well over a year. Dewey's reputation as a problem solver began back in elementary school, when his good friend Seraphina begged him to rescue her from her overprotective mother. One pack of powdered-sugar donuts, a stakeout, and some fancy footwork later, Dewey had freed his friend Seraphina and found himself a reputation. He soon got so busy helping kids solve their parent problems that he needed help. He enlisted his long-time babysitter, Clara Cottonwood, for the job. Together, with her own able-bodied furry assistant Wolfie, they established a suitable office space for clients hidden up in the attic of Dewey's home.

"Oh, sir. All set for you. See? That spreadsheet there. By topic. Teacher problems are there and the parent ones are over here," she said pointing.

"There is one," she continued, "I thought you might want to consider just due to the sheer number of times you've been contacted in our absence."

Dewey looked up for Clara to continue.

Clara sorted the document by name. "Twenty-seven times," she nodded seriously.

"Oh. Wow. Yeah—pull that info first, would ya?" Dewey sat back and began to crunch on an iced lemon cookie.

"It's a parent problem," Clara said. "The client is Archie. Tomorrow too soon?"

"For twenty-seven requests? Better make it yesterday," Dewey laughed as he packed up his stuff to head out. "Skijoring, huh? I could use a mode of transportation around town like that. Maybe we should fatten you up, dog, and I'll get a skateboard or some roller-skates. Not a bad idea. Throw him a cookie, Clara."

New Kid

When Dewey showed up at the vending machines the next day, Seraphina was hanging out with a girl who he'd never seen before.

"Dewey, this is Elinor."

"Hey," Dewey said.

"I met Elinor over break, but I didn't know she was going to go to school here."

"Me neither," Elinor shrugged. "My parents just decided to stay."

Elinor, whose father was Japanese American, had short dark hair; one side was cut shorter than the other, and there was one patch of pink.

Dewey tried to feed his dollar into the vending machine, but it kept spitting it back out.

"Argh!"

"Here," Elinor said handing him a crisp bill. "Try this."

"Oh, pretty!" Dewey said admiring how new it looked.

Seraphina looked up and flushed. She thought Dewey was commenting on Elinor, not the dollar bill. Elinor wore a bright four-tone vest, and her thin, bare arms hung by her side. She had a small nose with two perfectly symmetrical nostrils, should anyone care to notice such things. Seraphina thought she was pretty. Maybe Dewey had noticed that, too.

"Shame to put it in there . . . but . . ." He put it in and handed her his soggy wrinkled one in exchange. Out plopped a fruit leather and a quarter in change.

"Thanks. I wonder wh—" but he choked on his words as Colin approached him from behind and wrapped his arms around his throat.

As he coughed, he sputtered, "There you are!"

He and Colin began to head over toward the grass.

"You coming?" he asked Seraphina and Elinor.

"No, you guys go ahead." And they headed off in the opposite direction giggling together.

"Oh, great," Dewey said.

"What?"

"Did you not just see Seraphina go off with that new girl, Elinor?" Dewey ripped a bite off of his fruit leather.

"What new girl?"

"Are you—. What? Hello!?"

"How much time is left?"

"Dunno. Ten minutes?"

"Wanna go see if Mr. Peters is around? He's always good for a laugh."

"Sure, why not."

Dewey had forgotten all about his fake glasses! That afternoon as he waited for Archie to arrive, he settled them smartly on the bridge of his nose, and took a selfie, and then a couple more. *Not bad*, he thought. Still no Archie though, so he fluffed up the landing pillow and moved some cookies around on a plate. It was good to have Clara back, alright. Clients were back to entering through the ducts and sliding into the office with cookies hot out of the oven waiting for them along their way (so as to discourage any claustrophobia, she'd always said). Dewey had just popped one of those ginger babies into his mouth when Archie made his landing.

Archie Thomas was a sixth-grade student at his school. He had attended a different elementary school from Dewey, so he didn't know him all that well, but he certainly had seen him around with a pack of other sixth graders. Archie had brownish-red hair, fair skin, and tiny brown triangular and round freckles all over. Today he wore an oversized black t-shirt displaying the periodic table of elements in Minecraft.

"Hey, Archie. This is Clara, and I see you've met Wolfie." Dewey offered Archie a hand to pull him up off the lime green cushion on which he'd landed. Wolfie, who'd settled into Archie's lap, wasn't moving, though.

"Move, dog!" coaxed Clara with her hands on her hips. Dewey bent over and scooped him up, and Archie stood and shook Clara's hand.

"Nice to meet you," he said to Clara.

"I hope you'll pardon some people's less-than-professional conduct," she said, shooting Wolfie, still in Dewey's arms, a look. "Would you please sit down? We'll get you some paperwork and refreshments."

"Those cookies on the way in were so good! Did you make them?"

"She did!" Dewey said putting Wolfie onto his dog bed.

"Today's under-the-glass-domes were ginger snaps. I've got some shortbread bites coming out of the oven in just a few."

"Mmm," Archie sniffed the air in approval.

"So, tell me Archie. What brings you to my office today?"

"It's my parents. They're driving me crazy."

"Well, you've come to the right place." Dewey pulled out some paperwork for Archie to fill out. Dewey could feel, though, that Archie really wanted to talk about it, so he held back handing it over just yet, and waited for him to open up about the problem.

"They're ridiculously strict. They have a complete ban on electronics on weekdays. Can you believe that?" Archie's mouth hung open after he finished registering his complaint, as if the weight of his words still weighed it down. Dewey could see the remnants of Clara's cookies.

"Whoa."

"Yeah."

"Man, something really does smell good."

"I know. She's good." As if on cue, Clara walked back in with a plate of little cream-colored squares the size of sugar cubes, flecked with multi-colored sprinkles.

"Shortbread bite?" she offered.

"Thanks! Oh, man those are good!"

"Help yourself," she smiled. "More are in the oven."

Dewey grabbed a handful and shook them into his mouth as if they were dice.

"Oh, yeah! Great, Clara!" he barely got out without spraying. He stopped himself from speaking more until he'd chewed and swallowed.

"So, back to your problem. That sounds bad. Tell me more."

"Well, there's not much to say. They're complete tyrants. I'm not allowed to play any video games on school days. I do it anyway, of course."

"How?"

"I go to Sebi's or Judah's mostly. Or I'll use the school iPads at school at lunch, sometimes."

"Ha-ha! We do that, too!"

"I don't know. My mom's mostly the problem, I think. My dad just doesn't want to fight her on it. He uses his computer all the time. She likes to model for me not doing it, though, so it's no-electronics-all-around! Except Dad."

"Interesting," Dewey said, tapping his pen again the rim of his eyeglasses. "Let's have you fill out the paperwork and send it in. I'll have more thoughts for you after that."

"Okay," sighed Archie. It just seemed too good to be true that he could ever actually be a normal kid playing video games on a Tuesday at home. He'd come this far, though, so he put his hand out for the paperwork.

"Already emailed it to you," Dewey smiled. "Leaves your hands free for some cookies, if you want, on your way back out."

"Oh, I want," nodded Archie. "Can I have a couple more of those, though, too?" he asked, pointing his chin toward the plate of the small shortbread squares.

"Help yourself."

Somebody else must have thought he was being invited to help his fluff-ball-furry self, because Wolfie got up, gave a long bone-crackling stretch, and sauntered over to the plate of cookies.

"Ha-ha! Not you!"

"Can I give him one?" Archie asked Clara.

"Give that dog a cookie and he gets nuttier than an outhouse at a peanut festival."

Dewey and Archie burst out laughing.

"I'll take that as a no-go, then! Sorry, buddy!" Archie said, patting Wolfie on the head as he walked over toward the Gator Electric Motorized Lift System they used to lift clients back up to the air vents.

"Thanks, Dewey. Outhouse. Peanut festival! Ha-ha!"

"Okay, Clara," Dewey said, walking over to get a red bell pepper from the fridge and sliced a few pieces for Wolfie. "Sit, Boy. Good! I guess we're back in the business of solving parent problems. It's good to be back!" He gave himself a slice of red pepper as well. It was nice to break up the sweetness of the cookies sometimes with something else, and he gave himself and Wolfie another slice each.

"Yes, sir," Clara said. "It's good to be back."

Shoo Fly

Elinor wasn't at all sure she liked this new school, and frankly no one had given her a good reason why they had moved. She had gone to the same school in Washington since kindergarten. All her friends were there. Then, suddenly, they take a trip one summer and just decide to stay in California? It didn't make any sense to her, and she wasn't going to pretend to be happy about it.

"So, every time we go on a vacation now I need to wonder if we're actually going to be moving there?" she asked her mother.

"Don't be silly," her mom said as she set down a plate of steamy pancakes before Elinor. "Only the good spots."

Her mom sat down beside her and pulled off a piece of pancake for herself to nibble.

"Mmm. These smell good." Elinor didn't want to feel hungry or enthusiastic about eating, but her stomach didn't get the memo and rumbled at the smell of the sweet creamy butter melting on top of the warm cake already smothered in maple syrup.

As she ate, the ache in her belly began to feel less immense.

"Bacon?" she looked up.

"Yup." Her mom stuck a couple strips of turkey bacon in the microwave and returned with them, along with a steamy cup of coffee for herself. She slid the crisp bacon onto Elinor's plate, and her own knee under her chin as she settled back at the table.

"Have you made any friends yet?"

Elinor hated that question. So much pressure.

"I guess so. Seraphina's nice. Where's dad?"

"Early morning meeting. I'm driving you."

Elinor sighed.

"What, no good? I'm not a good drive-you-to-school person now?"

"No. It's fine. I don't care who drives me. I just don't want to go."

"Ah. I get that," her mom said, coming in to land on another little corner of pancake.

Elinor slapped her hand like she was a fly swatter coming down on a fly and laughed.

"Why don't you make your own?!"

"I'm trying to eat healthy!"

"Ha! Well, then, I'm trying to help you." Elinor smiled and shooed her away.

Then she cut her a piece with her fork, swirled it around in the syrup, and fed it to her mom.

"Thank you."

"You're welcome."

Duck and Cover

When Dewey got to school, he only had about one minute and thirty seconds before the final bell rang, so he made a beeline straight to class. When he walked into Mr. Jordan's room, there was a big paper sign in the doorway that made Dewey duck down to enter.

As he settled into his desk, he spotted Seraphina's new friend, what was her name, that new kid with the pink streak in her hair in their class. Funny, she must have been there yesterday but he hadn't even noticed. Kind of hard to miss that pink hair, too. People are like that, thought Dewey. You sometimes don't even see them until you've met them. Then they pop up everywhere.

"Okay," began Mr. Jordan. "You've all got your math journals."

No. No. No, I don't. I don't have my math journal. He never told us to bring our math journal.

Dewey raised his hand.

"Fairchild?"

"Can I go get my math journal?"

"Sure, Dewey. But first, can you walk over to the door and have a look at the big sign, the one that hit you in the head as you walked in here today? Anybody else need to go get their math journals?"

About three additional hands went up. No, there went four, including Elinor's.

"Right. We'll just have you all take a little field trip over to the door, gather round, and Dewey will read the sign aloud for us."

"'Don't forget your math journals today,'" Dewey smiled, showing all his teeth as the whole class busted out laughing.

"Rrrruuuunnnn!" Mr. Jordan stretched out the word and they all sprinted out the door.

"Oops," Dewey said to Elinor at the lockers.

"I don't even think I have a math journal," she said.

"Ha! I don't think he would really expect you to since you're new. You just got caught in our round up. It's just a lab book like this. You're supposed to bring it to class every day." Dewey pulled out a green and white science lab notebook as he shoved everything else that spilled out of his locker back in and slammed the door to stop the avalanche.

"Got it," she said, pulling a fresh journal out of her locker.

They ran back together.

When they got back to the door Dewey ducked under the sign again, but Elinor grabbed his shirt and pointed up.

Mr. Jordon had changed the sign.

"Are you reading this one?" it read. "Initial here: X."

"Yes, Mr. Jordan. Yes, I am!" Dewey whispered, and he rummaged around in his pocket for a pen.

He handed the pen to Elinor, who then also initialed it. Dewey sat back down and noticed that the other kids had not noticed the changed sign.

"Better, Fairchild. There's hope for you yet." Mr. Jordan walked by and thumped Dewey's journal with a pencil eraser.

When they got out of class, Dewey met Seraphina and Colin at the vending machines to get a snack and then head on over to the grassy area. Elinor was sitting drawing in her new math journal.

"Hey, Elinor," Seraphina said.

"Can I see?" Dewey asked as she looked up.

She held up the page. She had what looked like a bunch of sketches of girls and women. Some had green hair, some purple, some black and brown.

"Whoa," Colin said. "Those are good."

Elinor gave a closed-lip smile.

"Do you have any more?"

"Not in here," she said as she flipped the page. "Just a bunch of eyes." She showed them she'd been working on drawing large manga-style eyes.

"I wish I could draw," Seraphina said. "I can't even draw the rocks I collect well enough to identify them."

"That doesn't look so hard," Colin said sitting down next to Elinor.

She handed him her math journal and pencil.

"Hmm." He tried sketching out one of those very round eyes she'd done. "How can just two round circles filled in be so difficult? Wait." He erased. "Okay. It's harder than it looks."

"What do you call that style again? Anime?" Dewey asked.

"No, manga, right?" Seraphina answered. "Isn't anime just for animation and stuff?"

"Yup."

"It's Japanese. Elinor Mori. You're Japanese, right?" asked Dewey.

"Jewish."

The bell rang.

"Well, see you guys," Elinor said.

"Jewish?!" Dewey called after her.

"Jewish," she called over her shoulder and walked away.

Trippet

Name: **Archie Thomas**

Grade: **6**

School: **Woodbine Middle School**

Home Address: **2 Mockingbird Lane**

Best Entry to Your Home Without Being Noticed: **No idea. We have an alarm system.**

Top Three Hiding Places in Your Home: **My room, the laundry area off the kitchen, behind the couch in the family room.**

Siblings (names and ages): **Angelica, 15**

Pets: **cat**

Parents' Names: **Naomi and Tom**

Problem Parent(s) Cause You: **Won't let me play any video games on weekdays**

It had been a while since Dewey had done this kind of stakeout. An alarm system was definitely going to complicate matters. He texted Archie.

```
alarm . . . think you're going to have
to just invite me over
```

Just then, Stephanie stuck her head in his room.

"What ya doin'?" she asked.

"Not much. I was about to do some homework."

"Can you let me read you a poem I have to read for English?"

"Okay." This was new. Stephanie never came in his room for help or for any other reason unless it was to bug him, and even that she hardly did anymore.

"I need to practice in front of a live human." She took his pulse. "You'll do."

No one had to tell Stephanie to stay away from video games on school days. Not that she really liked them, but she liked her phone and her friends more, and no one had to tell her how to stay away from those because she liked being the best at school the most.

Stephanie's hair, more dark blond than brown these days, hung straight to her shoulders. She was growing out her bangs, and she parted them in the middle, framing her face like a tapered curtain valance. Her eyes were brown, almost honey hued, and when she smiled her cheeks raised, adding a third dimension to what might otherwise seem a more simple canvas. She had, as most her age did, the occasional blemish to show for all the internal flux of her developing self. Today, she wore a pair of blue overalls with a white t-shirt.

"Emily Dickinson's 'Because I Could Not Stop for Death.' Ready?"

"Yup," Dewey hopped up on his bed and sat crossed legged.

When she'd finished reciting, flawlessly, Dewey noted, he applauded. "What the heck is 'trippet'?"

"Tippet," she corrected. "No idea. I still need to look it up. Want to look it up for me?"

"'A scarf-like narrow piece of clothing worn over the shoulders.'"

"That makes sense."

"Um, if you have any slim idea what that poem is talking about, I guess!" laughed Dewey.

"Do you want me to explain it?"

"Why, no I don't. Did you actually pick that poem?"

"It was from a bunch to choose from. But I liked it."

"Why do you have to learn it by heart, though?"

"Don't I sound super smart that way?"

"I guess so?"

"That's why!"

"Oh."

"Thanks! Can I do it once more if I need to?"

"Sure. Hey, Stephanie? What if Mom or Dad told you that you couldn't do homework on weekdays. What would you do?"

"That's a stupid question. Why would they ever do that?"

"They wouldn't. But what would you do if they did?"

"I'd find a way to do it anyway, I'm sure. I'm a good daughter, but I wouldn't let them ruin my life if they went psycho on me."

"Right," Dewey said slowly.

"You're a nut, Dewey," Stephanie said, smiling as she walked out. "But thanks for your help."

Just then, Dewey realized that Archie hadn't texted him back.

He texted:

?

Still no reply.

Then it hit him. It was a weekday! He wouldn't see anything Dewey texted him at all.

Quiñceaneara

"Hey!" Dewey said. "Here you are. I've been looking for you."

"Oh, Hi!" Archie did not look up from his screen. He had a laptop and was mining some stone in Minecraft.

"I had no idea we could be doing this in here! Wait 'til I tell Colin!"

"What? Wait. Skeleton, hang on a—YES!" Archie clenched his fists in a "money-win" gesture and looked up from the screen. "Yeah. No one's ever here at lunch or if they are, they don't seem to mind as long as we don't get too loud about it."

"Show me your base."

"Here. It's an underwater house. But I need sponges."

"Oh yeah, those are super hard to find. Underwater. That's cool, though," nodded Dewey. "Hey, speaking of super hard. Since I can't text you you're super hard to reach, so let's set up now when I'm coming over to your house. You're allowed *friends* on weekdays, right?"

"We're not fanatics!"

"Okay, okay," Dewey laughed. "See you there tomorrow, then."

"Argh!"

"Or not?"

"Creeper got me!"

"Sorry!" Dewey patted him gingerly on the shoulder.

Archie had already respawned, and his eyes were glued back onto the screen.

"Right, then. See ya!" Dewey said, walking out.

When he caught up with Seraphina and Colin, they had just about finished eating and were out on the grass deciding how much they should reveal to Elinor about the vending machine crisis of last semester. They'd almost lost their vending machines, but thanks to the snack gods and their own ingenuity, they had saved them!

"We didn't even *have* vending machines at my last school," Elinor said. "We had a food truck and little food carts once a week, though."

"Hmm. Not bad," Colin said, "but I like to know it's there, waiting for me right where I left it, when I need it."

"Yeah, I guess so," Elinor said, "but options are more limited that way. We used to have wraps, and bagels with cream cheese, and good stuff."

"Oh! I could go for a bagel and cream cheese now," Seraphina said.

"You'd be surprised what they have in the vending machines in Japan," said Dewey. "They've got everything in those things!

"Speaking of which," Colin said. "You're Jewish? How are you Jewish? So, you're adopted, right?"

"Colin!" Dewey and Seraphina objected together.

"It's okay," Elinor said, her cheeks turning almost as pink as the stripe in her hair.

"So, are you?" Colin asked.

"No. Are you?" she smiled back.

"No," said Colin.

"I am," Dewey shrugged.

"No, you're not," Colin said.

"That's not funny," Seraphina said.

"I AM!" Dewey insisted.

"What?! No way," Colin said. "How did we not know that?"

"You never asked."

"Swear?"

"I swear! Ask my parents."

"What?! Dewey's adopted?"

"Maybe *your* birth parents are Japanese," laughed Elinor.

"Do you know who they are?"

"Nope."

"Do you know their names?"

"I forget."

"Do you know how old you were?"

"When I was born?!"

"When you were adopted!"

"Three days."

"Okay," Colin said, starting to believe him. "Well that's something!"

"I don't know. I used to know all of the info. I just forget. You can ask my parents."

"Do you mind talking about it?" Seraphina asked.

"No. Not at all," Dewey said truthfully. He'd always known his parents adopted him. They used to talk about it a lot when he was little, all about how they had gone to Texas when he was three days old and picked him up to be their very one and only Dewey.

He thought about back in fourth grade when they did those projects on family history and background. He wasn't quite sure what to do then, exactly. His mom said he could share the story of being adopted or he could share their family background of coming from Sweden and Poland. He decided to share the family background because that's what felt right to him.

One time in Life Skills, in third grade, Ariana shared her adoption story and Dewey had shared that he was adopted as well. So it was funny to think that not everyone knew, now. But it just hadn't really come up in middle school yet.

"Whoa. Dewey's adopted. That's so cool!"

"You kind of look like your mom, though, that's funny," Colin said. Dewey shrugged. Turning the conversation back to Elinor, Colin said, "So you are Japanese?"

"I don't think so," Dewey answered.

"Not you, doofus! Elinor!"

"Yeah."

"Why'd you say you were Jewish?"

"My dad's family is from Japan. My mom's born in Seattle."

Colin cocked his head, still confused.

"She's Jewish. I'm Jewish. I'm Japanese. I'm American. I'm a girl, not a rabbit."

"Oh! Why didn't you just say so in the first place?"

"He only asked if I was Japanese."

"That's true, Dewey. That's what you asked," Seraphina said.

Elinor flashed her a smile.

"Hmm," Dewey agreed, nodding thoughtfully.

"It suuure was," Colin agreed, drawing out the word.

"My dad tested his DNA to find out his genetic background. He found a whole bunch of his background came from Armenia. We don't even know family from there," Seraphina said.

"Well, this *has* been a very there-are-different-kinds-of-families lunch! I'm so glad you could all join us!" Colin said, sweeping his hands grandly.

"You're a goofball, Colin" said Seraphina, and they all laughed in agreement, standing up to throw away and recycle their trash.

"So do we get to go to your *quinceañeara* when you're thirteen?" Colin asked.

Seraphina, Elinor, and Dewey all burst out laughing.

"My *Bat Mitzvah*? Yeah, sure."

"Well, I'm sorry. I don't speak Hebrew."

"Have you learned nothing in Spanish? Quince. Fifteen?!"

"Huh. That's funny," Colin said, nodding slowly as he put the pieces together. "Well, can I still come?"

"Absolutely."

That's Something

Dewey sat at Archie's kitchen table having an after-school snack.

The house smelled warm and inviting when they walked in on what was probably the first rainy day of the year. Both boys were soaked down through their backpacks, and they'd spread out the contents by the living room fire for drying out.

Schools in southern California were not prepared for rain. Lockers were outside, which made for a wet situation during inclement weather. The passageways from one class to the next were also mostly outside, so kids who rarely ever needed an umbrella, and who would rather be caught dead than holding one anyway, found themselves drenched as they entered their classes.

Dewey, at least, had a rain slicker with a hood that kept him mostly dry, and his backpack didn't leak too much. But it sure felt nice to be indoors on this rainy day with the smells of fresh dough and hotdogs in the air.

"Do you like catsup, Dewey?" asked Archie's mom as she pulled out warm mini-pigs from the oven. She had made the dough from scratch with flour, milk, and butter and rolled each little mini hotdog in the triangle of dough, brushed with a bit of egg for glaze, and sprinkled with salt. Dewey wanted to eat the smell.

"I do," Dewey nodded.

"Grab some, Archie," she directed. "And get the carrot slices out, too, would ya?"

This was turning out to be a whole different kind of stakeout, thought Dewey as he munched happily on a carrot stick and dipped his mini pig-in-a-blanket into some catsup.

"So, how about you boys enjoy your snack and, well, do you have much homework?"

"Not much at all," Dewey lied. He really wanted to see what she offered up for them to do without electronics if there was no homework to be done.

"I've got some," Archie said not catching the clue. My fault, thought Dewey. I should have prepped him better. He popped another hotdog into his mouth.

"Well, I've got enough to keep me busy while you do

some," Dewey said working the dog into his cheek so he could speak.

"Okay," she said. "Go take care of your work and then you can hang out."

In fact, Archie had very little work that had to be done, and Dewey did some of his own, and then there they sat.

"What'cha wanna do?"

"What do you usually do?" Dewey asked.

"I don't know. Whatever."

"You boys all done?" his mom asked, coming in from the other room.

"Yeah. Can we watch a movie? It's raining."

"No. Find something else to do," she said, smiling, and walked out.

"See," he said.

"Hardcore," agreed Dewey.

"Come on, let's just go in the garage. We'll find something there."

Dewey could not believe Archie's collection of Nerf guns. There were four, 50-gallon plastic storage bins filled with Nerf guns and darts.

"Whoa! No way!"

"Yeah. I know. I have a lot now."

Dewey began to unpack the boxes.

"What's this one?"

"Cross Bolt Blaster."

"Oh! And this?"

"Sharpfire."

"Pass me some darts!"

"It's pretty wet out, Dewey."

"True. Hmm. Oh, Soakers, then! We'll just get more wet!"

"Okay!"

"Here. This box is all the water ones."

They dug through the box and pulled out about six super soakers, pistols, bottles, and, Dewey's favorite, the Chewbacca Bowcaster, and went to the hose to fill them up.

It was no longer raining, but the grass was wet and muddy, so they took off their shoes and socks as they each ran to their respective bases.

"Hey! No head shots!" yelled Dewey as he got pelted on his cheek by a hard stream of water.

"Sorry! I didn't mean to," Archie said, putting his right hand up in a sign of appeasement.

Dewey took that opportunity to pelt Archie in his outstretched palm then ran around behind him and soaked his back.

Archie ran away laughing and recovered his grip to shoot Dewey back. It began to rain again, but they didn't care. They were already getting all wet. Dewey ran around behind the play structure and climbed up the slide so he could shoot down at Archie. Archie laughed and shot back up. Dewey slid down the slide and got his pants all wet.

"That was a bad idea!" he laughed, looking at his wet bottom.

"Should we go in now?" Archie asked.

"Yeah," Dewey said. "As soon as I—" and Dewey opened the cover on his Chewbacca Bowcaster and poured the rest of the water on Archie's head.

Archie laughed and took off, chasing Dewey again. Archie dropped his nerf gun and grabbed a watering can that had filled with rain water. Lucky for Dewey it was heavy, and slowed Archie down enough for Dewey to escape back up to the top of the play structure.

"Truce?" Dewey smiled and flashed his teeth at Archie as the latter stood below wielding the watering can. The rain began to really come down hard now and Archie's face looked like the wet windshield of a car that needed to turn on its wipers.

"Truce!" Archie laughed, putting down the watering can.

Dewey, now completely drenched, slid down the slide because you can't get more wet than wet.

They headed back to the house. Dewey's hair was plastered to his head like spaghetti drained in a colander, and Archie's shirt stuck to the skin of his back. As they approached the door, Archie's mom spotted them.

"Whoa! Hang on there, Wild Bill and Jesse. We gotta clean you up a bit."

'A bit?!' thought Dewey as they dripped water all over the floor.

"Stay right where you are, please."

"Jesse?" Dewey whispered to Archie.

"James. You know Jesse James and Wild Bill Hickok. Some famous gun guys."

"Ohhh," Dewey said, nodding.

As he looked down at himself and Wild Bill he had to admit, it was impressive that she didn't seem in the least bit upset. His mom would have thrown a fit.

Archie's mom came out with four big towels, and some extra clothes.

"Dry off and change. I'll make you some warm cocoa. Dewey, you can borrow some of Archie's clothes. I think these will fit. Hose off your feet outside, fellas."

Even though they were already wet, the water felt cold and miserable, and Dewey began to shiver.

They went to separate quarters to change, and when Dewey came out, a new smell hit his nose. Popcorn. He was feeling kind of peckish about now, and a warm cup of hot cocoa sounded like it would hit the spot.

"Hey! Are those M&Ms in there?"

Archie's mom had heated them up into the popcorn. That was pretty much the beginning of the end for him.

Dewey didn't care if he never played another video game on a weekday ever again. He was moving in.

The salted popcorn and the warm melty chocolate inside of the candy shell of the M&Ms made Dewey feel a kind of comfort inside, kind of like an old friend coming to visit again.

Dewey decided to just go for it.

"Mrs. Thomas? How come you don't want your kids to have electronics on weekdays?" he finally decided to just ask. He'd been expecting Archie's mom to be some sort of psycho, but she seemed normal, super nice even. Maybe a direct approach would give him the information he needed.

Archie shot him a look that said—OH YOU DIDN'T?!

Just then Archie's sister Angelica came in the front door.

"Dry off and come join us in the kitchen," their mom said.

"Oh! Popcorn!" She grabbed a handful and put it into her mouth.

"Good day?" their mom asked.

"Yeah, okay."

Mrs. Thomas began to clear the table and as her back turned, Angelica flicked Archie on the back of the neck.

"Ouch! Why'd you do that?"

"What?" she smiled, already on the other side of the table sitting when her mother turned around.

"Grr," Archie growled.

"Archie?" Mrs. Thomas asked.

"Nothing," he moped.

Angelica threw some more popcorn into her mouth and munched.

"To answer your question, Dewey," Mrs. Thomas continued, "it's pretty simple."

Archie slid down in his seat.

"Do you know what the gray matter area of your brain is, Dewey?"

"Not exactly."

"Well, it's where you process things."

Dewey nodded. He was using his brain matter now. Yes, he sure was.

"Multiple studies show that there is a loss of tissue volume with video gaming. It gets smaller. Do you understand? Where there is Internet and gaming addiction going on, YOUR BRAIN SHRINKS. Do you want to know, Dewey," she continued, "where they have found this shrinkage?"

Dewey shook his head 'no.' Then realized he meant yes. He did want to know. "Yes, I mean yes. Where?"

"In the frontal lobe which has to do with your planning, organizing, and how well you and Archie here can control your impulses. But that's not all, is it, Archie?"

Archie sighed, putting his head down into his folded arms on the table.

"No, it also shrunk in the striatum. The striatum controls your socially unacceptable impulses. Do you know what that means?"

"I think so," Dewey said. "That means I don't put my feet on your kitchen table?"

"Or that I don't fart at yours," Archie said, lifting his head up and laughing a little.

She laughed. "That's true, too." At least she still had a sense of humor, Archie thought.

"Studies also showed," she continued, "that Internet and gaming addictions damaged the area of the brain that controls your ability to have empathy and compassion." She took a breath.

"Wow," Dewey said.

"I'm not done," she said sitting back down at the table. "That's just the gray matter. There are concerns about what studies show happens to the white matter, reduced cortical thickness . . . Dewey, do you want reduced cortical thickness?"

"Is that good or bad?"

"Bad! It's associated with doing poorly on tasks."

"Oh. No, then. I'll stay thick."

Archie dropped his forehead back down in the palm of his hand.

"And it's not just brain atrophy. Studies show video gaming makes you lazy, overweight—"

"I think he's got it, Mom."

"Thank you, Mrs. Thomas. This has been very informative. What time is it? I probably better get going now before it gets raining again."

"Oh, look at the time. It has been lovely having you, Dewey. I'll call your dad to pick you up soon. Why don't you boys go up to Archie's room until he gets here."

"Thank you, Mrs. Thomas."

"Anytime, Dewey. Anytime."

"What are those clothes?" his dad asked when Dewey got in the car.

Funny—even though he carried a bag of his wet clothes, he'd forgotten he had on Archie's.

"Oh! Right. *Amazing* Nerf war. Got totally soaked."

"The rain?"

"No, mostly water guns. Awesome!"

"Well, good! Glad you had fun. This a new kid? You've never mentioned him before."

"No. I mean yes, all sixth graders are new. He didn't go to our elementary, too, though."

"I see. Well, great that you're making some new friends."

"Yeah," Dewey said, but his thoughts were already somewhere else, thinking about what Archie's mom had said and needing to unwind from his long day. He pulled out his phone, which had been on silent in his backpack at Archie's house, to see if he'd missed anything. Nope. So he loaded up Clash of Clans and began to play.

"Um, what ya doing back there?" They had a long-standing no phone in the car rule, except on long trips.

"Aw, Dad. I haven't been on all day. I just wanna check on my troops. I'll lose my base if I stop now."

"Okay, finish this round and then put it away, please."

Funny, Dewey thought, how every family had its own rules. He could play it once at home but not in the car. Why?

When he finished his round, he asked, "How come I can't play on my phone in the car?"

"There's a world going by, Dewey. You'll miss it! There's a dad in front of you with scintillating conversation!"

"Not really," Dewey said. "I just stare out the window and do nothing."

"That's something, son. That's something."

Back-Up Brain

Dewey sat in his office, trying to piece together his visit with Archie and map out a plan of action.

"I wasn't expecting his mom to be nice," Dewey told Clara. "And we had an awesome time. I totally wasn't expecting that, either."

"So, what's the sticking point?"

"Her brain is obsessed about his brain getting ruined by video games. She's got this whole thing about your brain shrinking by playing too much, and it making you do stupid stuff, or how it makes you lazy or fat! But I know tons of kids who play all the time. I play during the week. Colin plays loads! Well, it's true, he's kind of a nutjob," Dewey said, laughing.

"So?"

"So, so, something isn't adding up."

Dewey went to the computer and looked up 'video game addiction,' 'video games damage brain,' and 'video games children obesity.'

"Umm," reported Dewey after about an hour of reading and a plateful of Clara's chocolate sandwich cookies. "Clara, I'm discombobulated."

What's wrong, sir?"

"I'll tell you what's wrong. She's *not*."

"Not wrong?"

"Right."

"She's right?"

"Right. She's not wrong. Clara!" Why was she getting so confused at this, perhaps possibly the most terrible news of his career? Not only was he going to let Archie down, his own brain might be shrinking. "I'm saying the studies do show some stuff."

"Like what?" Clara asked, rolling her chair up to Dewey's desk to get a closer look. Wolfie had been sleeping on her lap and jumped off, disturbed by her movement. He shook his whole body as if to shake the sleep off himself and drifted off to the corner to try and find it again.

"Well, all that brain stuff I guess is true. There are lots of articles and stuff that support what she's saying.

"That's good to know. Have you tried researching to see if there are counter-positions?"

"Good! Good idea."

"Always a good idea." Clara smiled and patted him on the head.

Dewey hunkered back down.

"Clara," he said when he came back up for air, "get a load of this. Did you know they did a study that shows that motion-controlled video games help with real world competition?!"

"That's the way, sir."

He went back under for more.

"Oh! Mrs. Thomas should read this article about how game controllers have changed over time and are used in the real world! The U.S. Navy is using a controller like the one we use in real life. Oh! Oh! In case she doesn't like real war stuff, look! They use the Xbox controller for MRI and CAT scans for medical stuff at one company because it works so well. They said it helps the surgeons prepare for the surgery!"

Dewey read on and on. The more he read, the more he found some articles that supported and others that contradicted Mrs. Thomas' position. His head began to swim and his eyes to blur.

He put his feet, which were up on the desk, on the

ground. The feeling of the ground under his feet helped to steady him. He sat up, took in a breath, and let it out.

"Maybe this article in the journal *Pediatrics* can help," he said hopefully. "It seems to say a little of both, I think. According to them, it's only a problem for kids who are . . . 'problematic video gamers'."

"Go on . . ."

"We only have a problem, if we, I mean, Archie, answers yes to ALL of these questions:

- I have been unsuccessful in cutting back.
- I experience an irresistible urge to play.
- I experience tension that is only relieved by playing.

"Do you think he'll be able to answer no to any of them?"

"I think so. He seems fine to me. Just a normal kid. Plus, there's a lot of fun stuff to do at his house. And good snacks!"

"I think you're onto something, sir."

Dewey let out a big sigh.

"I'm getting hungry." He looked at the time on his computer screen. It was almost dinner.

"This has been a productive afternoon!" Dewey said, pleased now that he'd come out on the other side of it with all he had discovered. He just had to figure out his next steps.

"What are your next steps?"

How did she always do that? Know what he was thinking? But Dewey's head was full and his stomach was empty. The energy from the cookies had burnt off long ago.

"Don't know. My brain hurts from thinking so much. I think my cortical thickness is reduced," he laughed.

"Why don't you go down to dinner, and Wolfie and I will give it some more thought."

"Okay, that's good. Thanks, Clara." He gave her a sleepy half hug, patting her back, and then walked over and distractedly pat Wolfie on his haunches.

As Dewey climbed out through the air ducts, his tired mind felt far away. He still had homework to do after dinner. It occurred to him what a wonderful thing it was to have a whole second brain, full of plump gray matter working on this for him. Clara was like having a back-up brain. When his got too full or tired, her back-up mind kicked in. He let out a breath that he didn't realize he'd been holding and made an audible sigh.

The smell of dinner hit his nose almost as quickly as Pooh wrapped herself around his leg when he walked through the door.

"Hey, Pooh!" he pat her on the head. She greeted him,

pretending to be a dog excited to see him at the end of the day. "Good boy," he said going along with her game. She panted.

"What's for dinner?"

"Arf!"

"Go fetch!" he said, throwing a pretend bone.

He walked in the kitchen, where the warm smells of dinner welcomed him.

"Oh, good, Dewey! Dinner is almost ready. Hungry?" his mom asked.

"Starving."

How Does Your Garden Grow?

The rain had stopped but the tables and grass outside were still sopping wet, so Dewey and his friends stood around the garden eating their lunch.

"Well, the garden got some water," Seraphina said. "That's good!"

"Good thing it didn't rain like that when we had all of Clara's cookies in there," laughed Colin. "That would have been a disaster."

With that remark, the cat was pretty much out of the bag, so they proceeded to tell Elinor all about last semester and how they had "planted" cookies, chips, and all sorts of snacks in the garden to protest the school administration's removal of their vending machines.

"It was beautiful," Colin said.

"Sure was," Dewey agreed.

"Here," Seraphina said, digging her phone out of her pocket. "I have some pictures."

Elinor mouth dropped open. "You guys did all that?!"

"We did, and it worked. We got our vending machines back."

"Nice!" nodded Elinor, scrolling through the pictures. "Oh! Ha! He's huge! Who's that?"

"Oh, that's my dog!"

"Peewee!" laughed Dewey.

Just then Mr. Peters walked by. "Yo, Johnson. Phone away or it's mine."

"Oh. Right. Sorry," she stuffed it back into her pocket. "I don't really get the harm in looking at some pictures," she said once he walked out of earshot.

"Me, neither. They should see what's going on with those iPads in the lab," Dewey said.

"Why? What's going on there?" Colin asked.

"Minecraft, for one thing."

"Oh! I gotta get in on that!"

"I know. We haven't played for so long. Why'd we stop?"

"I don't know. Our base's just sitting there. We should go back to it."

"Let's go see if anything's growing in there," Seraphina said, pointing her chin toward the garden.

The ground was dark and moist from the rains, and water still clung onto the green leaves of the arugula and spinach like little glass domes. Before a raindrop ever hits a leaf, water molecules, high in the clouds above, bond together in their small globular world. As they make their journey to earth, the bonded molecules sometimes bump into other downward drops and envelop them into their own microcosms. Colin, Dewey, and Seraphina, thick as thieves, with Elinor now part of their spherical little community, made their way through the muddy garden.

"The peas are starting to have pods!" Seraphina pointed to the trellises.

Colin tore off a piece of something green to taste it and spat it out. "Ach! It's bitter!"

"Ha! Mustard plant? Chard? Who told you to stick it in your mouth?"

"It looked good."

"It *is* good . . . mixed in a salad."

Elinor crouched amid a bunch of parsley-like greens and, wiping the dirt, exposed what looked like a bunch of orange coins. "The carrots are starting to come up."

"Cool! Let me see! Ugh. I have mud all over the bottom of my shoes," Colin said.

They all lifted a foot to see about an inch-thick clod of mud.

"Oops," Dewey said.

"Glad I wore my dark Vans," Elinor said.

Just then, of course, the bell rang.

"Take the field," Colin suggested. "We can drag our feet on the grass as we go."

That proved a bad idea, though, as the only thing muddier than the garden was the field.

"Oh boy," Dewey said.

"Oh boy," the others agreed.

Before tracking all that mud into his classroom, Dewey's science teacher stopped him at the door.

"Hold up there, mister," she'd said, and had him remove his shoes. He wasn't sure how the others had fared, but for his part, he'd taken science today in his socks.

Input Lag

A sock-footed Dewey made his way into the office to catch up with Clara again. After all this time, he'd never thought to remove his shoes coming through the vents, and it had a whole different feel. He found it easier to crawl along as the top of his socks slid over the metal.

When he got to the first cookie, he lifted the lid on the small glass dome. Today's sample was a chocolate crinkle cookie. A perfectly round chocolate cookie, studded with mini-chocolate chips and rolled in powdered sugar with a crackly exterior. Dewey popped the whole thing in at once and began to chew. It had a deep rich cocoa flavor, not too sweet but complex and satisfying. 'Molasses?' he wondered. Such questions would never have crossed his mind before meeting Clara. Now, he enjoyed trying to guess. Whatever it was, it was good.

"Where are your shoes, sir?" Clara asked when he landed onto the client pillow.

"Outside. Caked in mud."

"It does get muddy after the rains. Let them dry out and you'll be able to bang it off."

Dewey stood up. "Good cookies! Any more of those?"

"You know there are," she smiled.

"Hey, where's Wolfie?" Usually by now he would have run up and greeted Dewey.

"Groomer. He needed a haircut."

Dewey sat down at his desk with a plate of warm crinkles.

"Thanks! So, any more thoughts on Archie's case?"

"Just this one: game controllers in the modern world." She stood up and clapped her hands together in one solid gesture of completion.

"Huh?" He had no idea what she was talking about. Was that all she had to say?!

"That's it. You'll take it from there, Dewey!"

Now Dewey stood up too. "But I don't know what you're talking about."

"You do! I got the idea from you yesterday."

"Game controllers?" Dewey asked, squinting his eyes.

"Right." Clara gave a nod.

"Right, what?"

"Right, you got it! Now I'm going to fetch Wolfie. Back in a bit."

And she walked out.

"Ugh!" Dewey smacked himself in the forehead and sat down at his computer. He stared at it blankly. Didn't she promise to help him?

He pulled up those articles again about game controllers and the Navy, the medical world, and their effect on today's culture. Where did she want him to go with this? Dewey sat there tapping at a pad of paper with a pencil making a bunch of dots.

Nothing was coming to him.

He drew a t-chart and wrote "Problem" on one side. On the other side he put "Game Controller" since that's what Clara said was the answer to the problem. Then he added an "s" to the word Problem to make it Problems and started adding to the list:

-Archie = video games

-Mom = no weekdays

-A plays anyway

-She Ø thinks he's playing.

-She thinks A has problem (addiction etc.)

-A. Ø know how good has it (snacks! Nerf!)

Argh! He already knew all of this. And he was getting bored.

He wrote "Controller" again in the middle of its own page and circled it. He tried to do a brainstorm web, drawing long lines off of it and connecting words related to it. Well, he thought, let's see. Video games have controllers, obviously. He wrote that down. Archie's mom is a controller, he laughed to himself—with a big fat mother board. That cracked him up. She only thinks she's controlling everything, cause he's off sneaking around. That's a whole other kind of video controller! He smiled to himself. He didn't feel like doing these dumb school strategies. They weren't getting him anywhere other than amusing himself.

Dewey shoved a crinkle in his mouth. He was hoping to see Wolfie's new haircut, but he had homework and his math book was in his room. He left Clara a note: "Had to go. Back tomorrow. You left me with the controller, but I got some input lag."

Can You Feel Water?

"Who even knew he had eyes," had been Dewey's first remark. "They're very expressive." He smiled and stroked Wolfie's silky-smooth fur. His eyes were two glassy brown marbles with a big black bull's eye in the center. Fluttering above them were long, soft willowy black lashes. Dewey rubbed his forehead into Wolfie's fur. He smelled like vanilla and almonds.

The fur had been cleaned up around his mouth, and his whiskers were cut blunt and even. Dewey didn't know how he did it, but that dog smiled with his curled pink tongue.

"So, yeah," Dewey began. "I pressed and held the guide button to turn on that game controller you left me holding, but, uh, *no* connection," Dewey shrugged. "I made this stupid list," Dewey held up his stupid list. "Still nothing. So I consulted the user manual. It suggested I 'chat with a volunteer from the community.'" He sat down, folded his arms in front of his chest, and stared at her.

She laughed. "Okay, okay. Sorry I ran out on you, sir. He really was a furry mess."

"Well, that makes two of us now," Dewey said, running his finger through his hair anxiously. "Come on, Clara. I'm out here drowning."

"Let me see that list, sir."

She looked it over.

"But, sir," she said. "You're already doing it. You just have to find your feel for the water."

"Huh?"

"In swimming. They call it 'feel for the water.' It's when swimmers grab hold of the water and use it to propel themselves forward."

"How can you grab hold of something that isn't solid?"

"Exactly."

"Exactly, what?"

"Exactly, right. They feel how the force they exert against the resistance propels them forward."

"The force they exert against the resistance propels them forward?" he repeated.

"Exactly."

Archie slid onto the pillow with a flop, and a newly coiffed Wolfie ran to greet him with a happy pant.

Dewey looked at Clara, his eyes wide.

"Good to see you, boy!" Archie said patting him. Wolfie made some happy noises, and Dewey motioned for Archie to come in and sit down.

"Okay," Dewey began. "Here's the thing." Archie looked at him intently.

"Actually. Let's start here," Dewey began again. "Please answer these questions for me as true or false:

"One, 'I have been unsuccessful in cutting back video game playing.'"

"Well, no one has asked me to cut back? Unless you mean my mom asking me not to play on weekdays? Then I guess I have to say true because I have not been successful doing that."

"Interesting," nodded Dewey. "Okay," he continued. "Next one. 'I experience an irresistible urge to play.'"

"True, yes. I think so. I do. Sometimes, yes."

"Hmm. Okay. Huh. Last one. 'I experience tension that is only relieved by playing.'"

"Tension? What's that mean? No, I don't think so. That doesn't sound right. False."

It was touch and go there for a minute. Dewey let out a sigh.

"Good news. You don't have a video game problem. You aren't what researchers would call a 'problematic video gamer.'"

"Well that's good news!"

"Yup!"

"So, we just tell my mom that! And you've fixed the problem!!" Archie jumped up and clapped his hands together. Dewey wished it could be that simple.

"Somehow I think it may take a bit more convincing."

"Oh. Okay." Archie settled back into his chair. "You might be right about that."

"Here's the thing," Dewey felt his way through his words. Clara slid his list from yesterday back to him across the table and walked out. He glanced back down at it. Like a swimmer dipping his foggy goggles into the water to clear them, it began to emerge. Controller. *Controlling.*

"You and your mom have a problem. She doesn't want you to play video games on the weekdays. You're going to have to tell her that you've been sneaking it elsewhere."

"What?! NO! You're CRAZY!"

Clara came in with a plate of black and white cookies.

"You made black and whites?!" Dewey exclaimed.

The insides were soft cake-like cookies, the outsides half-frosted vanilla, the other half chocolate.

"Wow," Archie said. He took a bite right down the middle so he got both chocolate and vanilla in his bite. "Wow."

Dewey liked to eat all the vanilla first and then leave the chocolate half second.

"My dad would *die* if he knew you'd made these!"

"I'll save him some," Clara said. "I'll bring them around later today, or tomorrow."

"You gotta, Archie. It's the only way."

"Why?" he said, forgetting to chew his cookie. A swirl of black and white frosting and cookie crust sat on his wet tongue.

Dewey offered Archie another cookie. Archie distractedly bit into it, exacerbating the problem.

This kid needed to chew. "Well, buddy, it's like this. We need your mom to understand that she thinks she's controlling the situation, but it's not working.

"The *only* way to have her open to that without killing you for breaking her rules is if you're the one who cops to it. And, I think," Dewey said, feeling his way through his words, "if she finds out from somebody else, you're gonna get busted. This way, you confess and come up with a solution together. She's a reasonable person, right? She seemed like it the other day."

Archie worked out the cookie in his mouth and swallowed.

"Kind of. Yeah. I guess so. She's just crazy about this computer stuff."

"Okay, we'll take it nice and slow."

"Slow? How is confessing 'slow?!' What if I get in trouble?"

"Well," Dewey spoke slowly, "you broke the rule, right?"

"Dewey! I came to you for help, not to get into trouble!"

Sink or swim, thought Dewey, sink or swim. As if Clara's cookies could somehow channel her lessons to him, he swam. "My friend," Dewey spoke, leaning forward and grabbing a cookie like he'd found a precious shell, "It's like the cookie. It's neither black, nor white. It's the same with your mother. Not just her ideas, or your ideas. We will find the gray in the cookie!"

"The gray in the cookie? That sounds kind of gross."

"Hmm. Maybe not gray. But you get the idea, right?"

"Yes. I get that I'm about to get grounded for the next thirty years."

"We'll do this one cookie at a time. Have another?" Dewey offered the plate.

"Might as well," Archie said. "Could be my last."

Family Dinner

It had been a while since Colin had come for dinner at Dewey's, and Dewey's parents were giving him the once over.

"Did you go anywhere over break?" Dewey's mom asked him as she plopped some rice onto his plate. "Beans?"

"Yes, please. We went with my mom to San Francisco to see her sister's family."

"Oh, San Francisco is so great. Love the food at the Ferry Building. Right, Dewey?"

"Right!" Dewey said, biting into a taco. The bottom half of the meat dropped out onto his plate and he grabbed some chips to scoop it up.

"How's school?" Dewey's dad asked him.

"It's going great. Except science. Too much homework."

"I have homework," Pooh Bear said.

"Oh, you do, do you?" Dewey's mom smiled. "What do you have to work on tonight?"

"A paper for you to sign."

Colin and Dewey laughed.

Pooh frowned.

"Oh, no, Pooh. They're not laughing at you, right boys?"

"Right," nodded Colin. "I'd love to see your homework after dinner," Colin said patting her arm gently.

"Okay!" she smiled.

"Okay," he nodded.

They ate their dinner, sharing their day. Dewey's dad talked about his kids at school. Then Colin asked, "Hey, does Dewey know his real parents?"

Dewey's dad pinched Dewey's mom.

"Ouch, Don!"

"She's real!" Dewey's dad sang.

"What Don means, Colin," Dewey's mom said, rubbing her arm, "is that we *are* Dewey's real parents. You want to know if he knows his birth parents, though, right?"

"Oh, yeah, right! Sorry! I didn't mean—"

"Don't worry, nobody's hurting anybody here except Mr. Pinchy Fingers."

"Sorry! I didn't mean to pinch you hard! I was just playing!" He kissed her pinched spot.

"Yeah, yeah. I forgive you," she smiled. "No, he hasn't met them. Maybe someday if he wants to he will."

"Whoa. It's so cool. How old was he when you adopted him? Can I ask?"

"Sure. Of course. Dewey? You want to say?"

"No, you're doing fine," Dewey smiled. He liked when Colin asked the questions about it. They used to talk about it a lot when he was little. He'd always known he was adopted. They'd read books about how he was adopted, and they'd specially chosen him to forever be theirs. He'd never known anything else but this, though, so it didn't seem strange to him or even come up very often. But every once in a while it did, like when someone made an adoption joke in a movie or at school.

Once even his dad's second cousin who didn't know he'd been adopted joked about how his son must have been adopted as the punchline for something dumb he'd done. It didn't make Dewey feel bad. But it did make him feel different somehow, and remind him about being adopted in those moments.

His dad had taken his cousin aside and told him, and boy did that guy feel awful. He definitely felt worse than

Dewey did. It hadn't come up for a while lately, though, and he kind of enjoyed hearing his family and Colin talk about it.

"We adopted Dewey when he was three days old. We got him from Texas. He's our little Texan." Dewey's mom beamed.

"Wow. That's so cool," Colin said. "It's kind of weird, but he looks like you guys."

"Yeah, well Dewey has all my allergies to dust mites and cats, too," Dewey's dad said. "Life is funny that way!"

"I'm adopted, too!" Pooh Bear said.

"No. You're not. You were what we call a wonderful surprise!" Mom smiled.

"I'm a wonderful surprise!"

"I'll give you a 'surprise,'" Dewey said.

"Did you adopt Stephanie from Texas, too?" Colin asked.

"She's a wonderful surprise!" Pooh said.

"Not quite," Dewey's dad said to Pooh. "We have three children, two biological and one adopted and all real if you pinch them."

Dewey pinched Colin.

"Ouch!"

"This one's real, too."

They all laughed.

"Do we have anything good for dessert?"

"No, but I was thinking," Dewey's mom said, "When Stephanie gets home soon we can all go out for some ice cream before we take Colin home. Good?"

"Good!" Dewey said.

"Good!" Pooh Bear imitated.

Cyranose

Archie was terrified to tell his mother that he had been sneaking around playing video games during the week, and each day that Dewey found him at school to ask how it had gone was another day that passed without it going. Dewey instructed him to come by the office after school for a new plan of action.

When Dewey arrived at the office that afternoon, Clara had prepared Minecraft cookies for Archie. She had square cookie Creepers, Steves, Pickaxes, pigs, and sheep.

"Just when I think you can't be outdone!" Dewey said. "I didn't even know you knew what Minecraft was."

"I didn't. I looked up Mindcraft! Wouldn't that name make a lot more sense?"

"Not really. They're mining for things."

"Oh!"

"Well, whatever. You just made cookies too good to be eaten, they're so beautiful." He snapped a picture with #minecrafteats and posted it. "That ought to boost business!"

Archie slid in and landed on the lime green pillow.

"No time to waste, my friend. Let's get down to work." Dewey ushered him over to his desk.

"Whoa! No way!" He picked up one of Clara's cookies. "No. Way! Are these edible?"

"Of course. Always. Dig in."

Archie took a few snaps himself and then began to nibble on a Creeper.

"Just tell me what to do."

"Do you know who Cyrano de Bergerac is?"

Archie didn't.

"My mom read me a kid's book with it once. So, he's this guy back in the I-don't-know-when—a long time ago—who's got this huge, huge nose and loves this woman, but she's in love with this dumb good-looking guy who loves her, too, but he thinks he's too dumb for her. But Cyrano, the big schnozzle guy, is some great poet. So, even though he loves her, or maybe because he loves her, I can't remember—who even cares—he says he'll help the dumb guy and pretend to be him by writing stuff for him and whispering in his ear underneath her balcony. Are you following this?"

"Not at all."

"Basically, there are two guys. They both want the girl. Cyrano can write and talk great, but he's got the big nose. The other guy is a looker, but he can't speak worth two dead flies. So Cyrano whispers for him."

Archie laughed. "'Two dead flies!' But, I don't get it. Why would Cibaro do that for him?"

"Cyrano. Who knows why those guys did anything back then. The point is, I'm going to be your Cyrano."

"Are you calling me ugly?"

"No. I'm the ugly one! I'm Cyrano."

"Oh. So I'm stupid fly-guy."

"Yes. You're the stupid one."

"Sir?" Clara interjected.

"No. Wait. You're not stupid. My nose isn't the size of a dill pickle. I'm just trying to get our roles down. Have a cookie. The point is I'm going to help you talk to your mom when you get stuck. It's been almost a week, and we're getting nowhere fast. So, I'm going to whisper in your ear what to say when you get stuck. I'm going to give you some notes to get started, some talking points, and then, I'm going to speak to you like those newscasters in your ear."

"No way."

"Yup."

Dewey held out a tiny ear bud on his finger.

"See this? It hooks up with my cell phone. As long as you have it in properly you'll be able to hear me. Keep your head upright so it doesn't fall out."

"Whoa."

"I know, right? We'll be using technology on a weekday to break it to her that you've been using technology on a weekday. We're getting in deep!"

"Cool."

"Oh, yeah. That, too. Okay. At 16:00 hours tomorrow we 'meet' in your ear."

"I'll be there! Hey, if my nose was really as big as that Cyranoses guy's nose I could hide it in there instead of my ear," chuckled Archie.

"I'm the Cyrano. I'm the Cyrano. You're the other guy."

"Oh. Yeah. Right. Got it."

"Have a Creeper for the road."

Archie's House

Dewey sat impatiently after school waiting for Archie to "show up." They had already paired Dewey's cell phone with the device and practiced how to put the Bluetooth transmitter under Archie's shirt. It wasn't the technology side of things that had Dewey worried.

"Don't fidget with it or she'll know something's up. Don't touch your ear. And whatever you do, don't answer me! Just pretend I'm not in your ear."

As Dewey waited for his cell phone to ring, he regretted that they hadn't practiced more. Or at all! He paced the room, walking around the perimeter in a square and checking his phone to make sure he hadn't missed the call.

At 4:33 his phone rang.

This is it, thought Dewey. He put in his ear buds and gave Clara, who was in the kitchen, a thumbs up so she'd keep Wolfie out of the way.

"Not much," he could hear Archie saying. "Just some math problems."

"Okay, good. I can hear you loud and clear," Dewey spoke. "If you can hear me clear your throat."

"Ahem."

"Perfect," Dewey said.

"Now tell her you want to talk."

Nothing.

Dead air.

"Say, 'Mom, can I talk to you a minute?'"

"Mom, can I talk to you a minute?"

"Sure, what's on your mind, Arch?"

"Okay," Dewey directed into Archie's ear. "Sit down now if you're not already."

"Mom, sit down now if you're not already."

What?! No!! He was repeating aloud the directions Dewey gave him.

"Huh?" his mom asked. "Is there something wrong, Archie?"

"Listen, Archie," Dewey said slowly and carefully, "don't say this aloud. Only repeat out loud to your mom if I state 'SAY' first? Okay? If you roger that, clear your throat."

"Ahem."

"Good."

"Archie?"

"Say, 'Sorry, Mom. I think I'm just feeling a little nervous.'"

"Sorry, Mom. I think I'm just feeling a little nervous."

"What's on your mind?"

"Okay," Dewey whispered. "See what you can do. I'll help you if you get stuck."

"Mom," Archie began. "I know you don't want me playing video games on weekdays."

She arched her brows. "You know I don't."

"Well, the thing is," Archie hesitated.

"Go on," Dewey encouraged.

"The thing is I really want to."

"Good," Dewey said.

"I'm sure you do," she said. "But that's not how it works around here."

"The thing is," Archie said. "The thing is," he repeated.

"The thing is, I'm doing it anyway," Dewey said.

Silence.

"Oh. Shoot. SAY, 'The thing is, I'm doing it anyway.'"

Dewey could hear Archie swallow.

"The thing is, Mom, I'm doing it anyway."

"Nice," Dewey said, but it was hard to make it out over Mrs. Thomas' GASP that stretched out four syllables long. If she wasn't sitting she must be now, Dewey thought.

"How is that even possible?" she demanded. "Where? In your room?"

"No, but pretty much everywhere else."

"Well, you can just march up to your room, Mister. You've just lost your electronics for the rest of your life."

Now Dewey could hear a gulp, a door slam, and silence.

"Archie. Archie. Don't worry buddy. It's all part of the plan."

"She's really mad," Archie said into his ear.

"Yeah. But that went fine." Dewey assured. "We're moving onto phase two while you're in prison. Go charge that earpiece so it's ready to go."

When Dewey "hung up" the phone, if that's what you can call ending a conversation between the inside of your ear and someone else's, Dewey felt the weight of responsibility bearing down on him more than usual. How could he just go home now and eat dinner, do homework, and play a video game himself knowing that Archie was stuck? He at least needed to know that he had this sealed up airtight to bail poor Archie out.

He looked at the time and sighed.

"Clara, we gotta figure out our next steps before I go home tonight. I left Archie held captive in his room like a prisoner."

"How did his mother respond to his transgressions?"

"Oh, she sent him to his room and banned him from video games for the rest of his life."

"Oh, my. Well, she may need a little cooling off period."

"I told him to expect to be punished for it. I just didn't expect it to be forever!"

"That is a tad lengthy."

"Plus, I gotta help figure out our way through the rest of this mess."

Dewey wanted to stay longer and talk more with Clara, but he'd already pushed the time as far as he could and needed to get home for dinner. Once again, he found himself up in his own room with his own thoughts trying to make sense of it all. He sure hoped that Archie was having a better night's sleep than he was. He feared he was not.

Dewey Fairchild, Moptart Problem Solver

The next day in school Dewey looked for Archie in the lab at lunch, but didn't find him there. As he walked back out, Colin intercepted him.

"Hey, come on. We're all over on the grass catching up with Seraphina about some new rare rock she found."

"Ha! That sounds amazing!" Dewey laughed. "Hate to miss that one! I gotta try to find Archie, though."

"Oh, that redhead kid? I saw him over on the grass with some sixth graders."

"Oh, okay, then!" Dewey picked up his pace in that direction.

Seraphina waved him over, but he put up a finger to indicate he'd be over in a minute and walked over to Archie.

"Archie! Catch me up!"

"Oh! Dewey! Guys! Meet Dewey, leader of the free world! Moptart and Poptart Potentate!"

They all knew Dewey already and just laughed, figuring Archie referenced Dewey's well-known love and rescue of the vending machines.

Dewey sat down but jumped up as a cold wet spot on his butt began to announce itself.

"Aren't you getting all wet?" Dewey asked, pulling his pants away from his bottom and looking to see how damp it looked. Archie lifted his butt cheek and showed a plastic sandwich bag he'd been sitting on.

"Oh, great," Dewey said, pulling his pants away from his bottom again and trying to air himself dry. What was it about Archie and Dewey's bottom getting wet?

"Never mind all that, let's catch up. Come with me, though? I still need somethin' from the vending machines before the bell rings."

"Oh, yeah. Sure thing."

"Did we ruin your life?"

"What? No! You saved the world from destruction. I got captured, but we escaped world domination!"

Archie thought she'd come at him like some sort of frightful zombie. In fact, she had a lot of questions about how and where he'd been playing. But she also really wanted to understand better why.

"I showed her those three questions you gave me to prove I'm not addicted to video games. That scored me some points. Then Angelica admitted she texts during the week. Duh. Of course she does."

"So, you're not stuck in the nether??"

"We leveled up, Dewey! New family plan. 'A compromise', she said. Some games and social media during the week. No sneaking."

"Nice. That's great," Dewey said, remembering his hunger again. "Want some?" he asked offering some crackers as they headed back.

"No thanks," Archie said, reaching into a baggie of homemade Sriracha popcorn. "You?" he offered. "It's kind of spicy."

Dewey grabbed a handful and shoveled it into his mouth. Then he made a beeline to Colin's water bottle on the grass.

"Bring back my stuff tomorrow, Archie! And a bag of that popcorn! That's amazing!"

As he gulped down some of Colin's water, suddenly, Dewey got it.

Oh! Ha-ha! Dewey laughed to himself, wiping water off of his chin. 'Moptarts and Poptarts!' Parents!!

Memeing

Dewey woke up the next morning, found himself unusually rested, and wondered if it was Saturday. No such luck. When he came down to breakfast everyone was already at the table eating. Dewey's dad and Pooh had some sort of grain toast with avocado, Stephanie had an omelet, and Dewey's mom sat working on a cup of iced coffee.

"What'll it be, Dewbert?" his mom asked, looking up with a straw still in her mouth as she sipped.

"Can I have eggs?"

His mom glanced at the clock.

"Yup." She started cracking them into a bowl. "Scrambled?"

He nodded yes and slipped some sourdough into the toaster.

“Me,” Stephanie said, by which she meant, ‘Throw some in for me, too, please.’

Dewey’s dad began clearing the dishes. The toast popped, and Stephanie grabbed her slice, slathering it with butter and throwing her backpack over her shoulder.

“Hey!” Dewey’s dad objected.

She came back, gave him a kiss, blew her mom another, and flew out the door.

Dewey buttered his toast and sat to eat his warm eggs.

“Do you think Sriracha would be good on eggs?” he asked.

“You like Sriracha?” Dewey’s dad asked. He pulled out a bottle of the hot sauce.

“Oh, yeah. It’s great,” Dewey said, like he’d been using it his whole life.

“Oh, go easy, Dewey,” his mom said.

“I know,” he said drizzling a bit on his eggs.

“Dad, will you drive me so I’m not late?”

“Yeah, okay. Ready in five?”

“Yup.”

With a warm breakfast in his belly and a ride to school, Dewey felt on top of his game. He remembered his math journal. The vending machine didn’t have any problem digesting his dollar bill. This day was looking good.

As he sat in Humanities, he began to daydream about how exciting it was to do parent problems again. He had missed the stakeouts that come with parent problems, even if this last one had been more stake-in than stake-out. Dewey had a backlog of both parent and teacher problems waiting for him back at the office. He and Clara agreed they'd take a couple days to let her organize them, and then he'd meet her back in the office to go over their options and prioritize.

Dewey felt the back of his shoe being kicked.

"Dewey!" Colin whispered.

"Fairchild!" his teacher stared at him. "Where are you?"

"Oh, here!" he said flushing hot.

"Welcome back, then. As I was saying, before I was so rudely drowned out by the loud voices in Dewey's head, three memes are due tomorrow. You may work independently or with a partner if they have read the same book as you. Any questions?"

"Ha-ha!" Colin laughed at Dewey's classroom mishap when the bell rang. "We're working together, right?"

Dewey and Colin had to create three memes of one important scene from their book. One had to be an existing meme that they could argue relates. The second had to have the same picture but with the text from the book. The third had to have their own picture with the original text from the book. The only other part was that to get the "joke" or "punchline" or "message" of the meme, it had to meet the "only-those-who-have-read-the-book-get-the-reference" test, their teacher had said. He emphasized that *that* was the most important part.

"Isn't it obvious that you'd have to have read the book?" Colin asked. "That's the whole point."

"I'd think so," Dewey agreed.

"Whatever, let's just pick our scene. When he finds that weird box?"

"Sure."

"Or, no. When he swims too far in the lake."

"Yeah, yeah, that's good. Use that."

"Okay, hang on. Let me find it . . . Here: 'Jedd went with Ramona to the edge of Blue Lake. The water felt cold and goosebumps covered his bare arms and chest. Ramona hung back letting the water splash her ankles, but Jedd wanted to impress her so he plunged in quickly below his shoulders. The water felt refreshing now.'"

"Read ahead a little," Dewey said.

"K. Let's see. '. . . Tried to touch his toe to the bottom . . . How had the horizon and Ramona gotten so far, so small . . .' Okay, how about here, '. . . and all that Jedd could see was water. The lake's blue looked dark. Black as night. Treading water, he felt a thousand miles out, nothing on which to stand, rest, or lean.' Stop there?" Colin asked.

"Yeah, that's good."

"How's this?" Dewey laughed. He'd found a meme of an astronaut floating lost in space. As he tumbled head-over-heels, the text below read, "There's no Wi-Fi up here."

After they finished laughing they plugged it into the "does it meet the only-those-who-have-read-the-book-get-the-reference?" test.

"Well," Colin said, "It's funny 'cause space is black and so was all that water when he swam out that far. And he's floating around in it."

"Okay!! Okay!! Good! Meme generator. Get the line from the book."

"Use, 'He felt a thousand miles out, nothing on which to stand, rest or lean.' It totally works!!" They both laughed loud and hard, picturing that astronaut in space rolling around as that poor Jedd kid from the book.

"Okay, okay. One more. Now we have to use that same line but make our own meme photo for it."

"Look through your phone for pictures," Colin said as he began to scroll through old pictures on his own.

"You can search. Put 'water.'" Dewey said.

"Ha!" Colin pulled up a picture of them from a couple summers back—him, Dewey, and their friend Walker hanging on a raft. Dewey was wearing a short sleeved green rash guard, and the other two boys were bare on top.

"I still had braces, then!"

"Oh! Look." Dewey showed Colin a picture of a wet Wolfie dog-paddling in the middle of a sky-blue pool. Most of his body was submerged fully under water, but his wet black ears hung drenched, dragging on the surface. His usual fluff-ball hair lay flat, except for one piece of white fur that stood up on his snout like a compass guiding the way. That big black teddy bear button nose periscoped out of the water as he dragged a heavy waterlogged Skunky to safety.

"Aw, Wolfie."

"I know. Clara had to give him swimming lessons."

"With a class?" he laughed at the idea.

"Private lessons! Some dog swim school. They said he knew how but he was just scared, haha. The only way to get him in the water was to throw in his Skunky. Now, get near a pool and she says he drops Skunky in."

"This totally works! It'll be hilarious!" Colin stretched Wolfie bigger with his finger. "We'll just Photoshop in some water so it's dark. It's perfect. He's dog-paddling. That's totally treading water!! Look," he said, holding up the phone. They both laughed.

"Airdropping." As Dewey did so, however, he got a text and he and Colin both jumped.

A-oo-gahh.

"Could that be louder?!"

"Sorry. Didn't know I had it up so high," Dewey laughed as he looked down to see what Clara wanted. That was her text notification.

Boss. Better come by if you can. Now-ish good?

"Hmm. Clara wants me. That's weird. Finish up?" Dewey asked, flashing him a smile.

"Yeah, yeah."

"Thanks, pal!"

Dewey threw his stuff into his backpack and looked at his phone to make sure she hadn't written anything else. But that was it. He wondered what was up.

Discovered

Dewey slid into the office onto the pillow and could hardly process what he saw. At first, for all of about three full seconds, he thought everything was normal. His body did not register a crisis. Then, by about the fourth second, his body felt the tingling zap of a shock, like when someone jumps out around a corner and scares you unexpectedly.

He caught his breath. He made a quiet but audible gasp. His face flushed and got hot. His fingertips and legs buzzed. All that happened on second number four. And by second number five his brain caught up—Pooh Bear sat in his office chair, crunching on cookies.

He looked at Pooh. He looked at Clara.

She gave him a big shrug and a cheerful, "Look who slid in, boss."

"Uh, hey, Pooh, what ya doin' here?" Dewey spoke slowly.

This was a disaster of epic proportions. Dewey had to handle this situation delicately, but with his heart pounding in his chest, what he felt like doing was shoving her back up the air ducts.

How had she discovered their office?

What did she want?

She was going to ruin everything.

She slid off Dewey's chair, wiping cookie crumbs from her fingers onto her shirt, and began to wander around.

"I want to slide down again!"

"Pooh, how did you get here?"

"Through there!" she pointed at the air ducts.

"No, I know," he said, holding onto her shoulders and looking into her eyes. "I mean, how did you get the idea to go in there?"

"I watched you!"

Ugh! Dewey had thought he'd always been so careful.

Wolfie came over and began to lick the flavor of cookies off Pooh's fingers, making her laugh. She sat down on the carpet to pet him, but he walked away.

Suddenly, it occurred to Dewey his parents might start to worry and look for her.

"Pooh. Where do mom and dad think you are?"

"With you, silly."

"Why do they think that?"

"I told them I was going upstairs to be with you."

"Clara? Help me."

"Well, sir. I presume they think you are home and up in your room with her. Why don't you two go do just that until you and I can put our heads together about this, shall we?"

"Okay. Good. Yeah. That's good."

"Pooh. You can have another cookie, and we're going back to my room to hang out there. You can sit on my bed and be with me."

"Okay. I wanna come back here tomorrow."

"Maybe. I don't know. We'll talk about it later."

"Dewey, can I go down the slide again?"

"Not now. It's getting late."

"Tomorrow?"

"Maybe."

"I WANT TO GO DOWN THE SLIDE! WHY CAN'T I GO DOWN THE SLIDE!"

"Okay! Okay! Tomorrow. We'll find a time."

Dewey looked at Clara, his eyes wide.

They hopped up on the Gator, and Pooh let out a squeal of delight. As it rose Clara said, "You know, we can't always control what happens, boss."

"I can see that," Dewey grumbled.

"Sometimes, we can only control how we respond to what does," she called out.

On that, Dewey and Pooh made their way out, with Pooh enjoying little matcha-white chocolate sugar cookies along the way, and Dewey's throat too dry and constricted to even think about popping a cookie in his mouth.

Reacting

Dewey and Pooh went upstairs to his room without incident. His dad was either in the garage or not home yet, and his mom was busy on the computer and had not heard him quietly open the door.

Dewey would have liked to plop down on his bed, but it was occupied territory, invaded by a three-foot-five-inch, forty-one pound, long messy brown-haired almost six-year-old.

"You wanna color on paper or my iPad?" Anything to keep her busy.

"iPad!"

He opened a drawing app for her and sat down at his desk to try and think.

Impossible. He could not get past the chatter in his head, even with her totally quiet.

He texted Colin hoping for a distraction.

`how's it coming?`

Colin sent back the picture of Wolfie in the middle of the pool with Skunky in his mouth, only now, instead of the light blue water with ripples of white light, the water looked ink black and navy blue. Colin had placed Wolfie, smack dab in the middle of it and the caption read, ' . . . and all that Jedd could see was water. The lake's blue looked dark. Black as night. Treading water, he felt a thousand miles out, nothing on which to stand, rest, or lean.'

Dewey laughed aloud and sent back the cry-laughing emoji.

"What's funny?" Pooh asked.

"Somethin' for school."

"I have something funny," She held up the iPad. He smiled, nodded, and she went back to work.

He looked at the meme again and it made him smile for real. Dewey sighed.

"Guys, dinner," their mom called.

"Hey, Pooh. Let's just keep this slide and office thing between us, and then I'll let you come back with me tomorrow, k?"

"Yup," she said hopping off his bed.

"Good," he patted her on the head. "Good."

That evening, after he'd cleared the table, he went up to his room and plopped onto his bed. Finally, some time to think. He checked his chats and texts.

One asking for help had come in from Archie. He hadn't expected that again so soon.

Archie: `help`

Dewey: `your mom?`

A: `my sister wants to kill her now`
`HAVE to see you tomorrow`

D: `my office right after school`

Archie's sister? She was in ninth grade. Wonder what that's about, thought Dewey. Then he began to angst about how to get Pooh Bear her slide time and Archie his meeting time.

`4:30 instead one client before you`

He got the thumbs-up back.

What was it that Clara had said to him? You can't always control what happens but how you remix? Recycle?

Re-something. The whole thing was feeling re-diculous to him right about now. He still couldn't figure out how Pooh had even found him out. Argh.

He rolled over, put the pillow over his head, blindly felt around to turn off the light, and went to sleep without brushing his teeth.

Same Parent Problem Solver

Turned out, Pooh Bear wasn't even an issue that afternoon. She had a karate lesson after school. Dewey watched Pooh, all smiles in her little white karate *gi*, as she and their mom pulled out of the driveway. She waved goodbye to him from the back seat, without so much as peep from her about their previous plans.

That's not the only thing that didn't go as planned that afternoon. At 4:30, Archie did not show up to Dewey's office. His sister Angelica did.

Angelica Thomas was a ninth-grade student in high school. He'd never actually met her before, other than for that brief few minutes at Archie's house. Angelica's chestnut brown hair was knotted on top of her head in a bun. She wore two round gold hoop earrings and strands of hair fell here and there. She wore a plain white t-shirt and a warm wrap-around sweater she'd found at a thrift shop. Her eyes were blue and some days she wore a navy-blue mascara to accentuate them. Today, though, she wasn't wearing any. She didn't have the freckles that her brother Archie had. Come to think of it, neither did his mother. She did have a fair number of blemishes that looked especially red against her very fair skin.

"Angelica! Hi. We were expecting Archie." Dewey immediately regretted that'd he'd said so.

"I know. Sorry. When he told me about you, I told him I wanted to come myself. You guys have ruined my life!"

"Cookie?" Clara offered.

"This is Clara, and this is our office companion, Wolfie," Dewey said remembering his professionalism.

"Nice to meet you," Angelica said to Clara and Wolfie as if they were both people.

After Clara had offered the cookies, Angelica sat and her demeanor seemed to soften a bit.

"Oh, I saw cookies on the way in! I wasn't sure if it was okay to eat them."

"Oh, of course," Clara said. "Are the notes along the way not there today?"

"Could be. I'm just so stressed, maybe I missed them."

"Understandable," she assured. "How about having one now, and Dewey will hear all about what's on your mind."

"Well, I don't know, I—Oh," she interrupted herself. "These are good!—I don't know," she continued, "*what* you guys did to my mom, but she's suddenly all over the Internet and up in my business."

"Oh. Umm hmm. I see. This is an interesting development," Dewey said, sliding on his fake glasses. "So in fixing his own problem, it seems, Archie may have created one for you?"

"Yes. Yes, he has. It's horrendous!!! Now we all have 'designated family computer time'—including her!"

Dewey nodded slowly, taking it all in, and slowly adjusting his fake glasses.

And then, something happened that had never happened to Dewey in all his many, many months of problem solving. Angelica began to cry.

"It's just—choke-slobber—sob—so—choke-slobber—sob—beyond—choke-slobber—sob. She 'likes' her own posts! She, she comments on all the stuff I post! I, I seriously, I can't even talk about it. You guys have ruined my life." She broke down convulsing and sobbing into the crook of her arm on the desk. Thankfully, Wolfie came up under her and began to lick her tears, which made her smile and laugh. Dewey took that as his in.

"I can see you're upset. Who wouldn't be? It sounds awful. Try not to worry! You've come to the right place! We can fix this, or my name isn't Dewey Fairchild, PPS. And er, it is. So, I can. So here," he smiled, looking around for a tissue, but settling for a napkin instead. He handed it to her followed by a cookie. "We just need to tweak this solution a bit to take you into account."

"Archie might have done *that* in the first place."

"Yes, I suppose that's a good thing to keep in mind," he gave Clara a quick smile.

"It's not just me, you know—it's all my friends."

"Right," nodded Dewey. "Social media—the whole world sees it."

"YES!" she blurted out.

"I understand. I need your mom's social media passwords."

"I don't have those!"

"Right. Okay. But you follow her and she follows you on all of her stuff, right? So I'll just shadow you and see what she's doing that way. Anything extra she does I might not see, just take a snapshot for me.

At that, Angelica let out a sigh and nodded.

"Okay?"

"Okay," she agreed.

"I got this! Don't worry!"

Angelica nodded again and smiled.

As Angelica made her way back out through the air ducts, she lifted the little glass domes and ate some more cookies along the way. "Oh!" She thought to herself. "Look at that! Those little notes were here all along!"

#Don't #forget #to #floss

Dewey sat on his bed, scrolling through Mrs. Thomas' Facebook posts in Angelica's profile. Like most kids their age, Angelica didn't seem to be using Facebook all that much, but Dewey could see some of the things that might make Angelica not so happy. He chuckled at a #TBT of her where she'd stuck her tongue in the sand and it was covered like a cupcake in sprinkles. The caption read, "A. stuck her tongue in the sand for a boy she was swooning over in kindergarten." It had seventy-five likes and too many comments for Dewey to read. Another picture had Angelica's mom dressed in yoga clothes doing a head stand, followed by a video clip of her jumping up on some floor block thing and jazzercizing or something. Dewey cringed.

He switched to her Instagram. Angelica's was private, so he sent her a request, but her mom's was public access, so he started to look through her posts. She had the same exact photos there as she had on Facebook. Evidently, she didn't get that people would then just see the same thing twice. Then he started to laugh. '#Love #my #daughter #so #blessed', her mom wrote under a picture she'd posted of her. Um, clearly not getting the hashtag thing, he chuckled. He poked around some more.

"Oh, too good!" he said to his phone as he sat up taller. "She liked her own post here! That's pretty funny!"

Dewey yawned, and decided he would shut down his phone for the night. Just then, Angelica accepted his friend request.

So, instead, he started poking around. Without fail, every picture Angelica posted, her mother's comments were now among the first. "That's my sweetie!" or "Cute!" Sometimes though, and Dewey was pretty sure this must have been even more embarrassing, her comments had nothing at all to do with the pictures. "What time are you coming home from practice?" or "Did you finish your homework?" Dewey sighed. He wished it wasn't so late and that his eyes weren't closing on him, because there was a lot more material to sift through. He tried to look at some more but realized the comments began to blur with thoughts in his sleepy head and made no sense, so he called it a night. Just then his dad came in to tuck him in.

"Did you wash up, Dews?"

"Tonight?"

His dad laughed. "Okay. We'll try it your way. Did you wash up this evening, Dewey?"

Dewey sighed and hauled his tired body out of bed to go brush his teeth.

"Don't forget to floss," his dad called behind the door from his room.

Dewey hadn't forgotten. He had hoped his father had, though.

As he flossed his teeth, he sat on the toilet wishing he could be watching something while he worked. Flossing and brushing were so boring. He'd like one of those little tv sets in the bathroom mirror like in the fancy hotels. By now, you'd think they'd have computer screens just built right into them with touch screens. They probably already do at some of those really swanky places, he thought.

He sat back down to brush his teeth again, but this time he lifted the lid up so he could just spit between his legs straight into the bowl. That didn't go as planned, though, and he hit the lid and had to wipe it up with the toilet paper. Yeah, he thought. Touch screens in the mirrors. And he rinsed and spit.

His dad sat on the foot of his bed waiting for him.

"It's kind of late, so I think you should just go straight to bed. Let's work on getting this show on the road a little earlier so you can read a bit before bed, okay, partner?"

"Sure, Dad," agreed Dewey. "I could also save a few minutes if I skipped flossing."

"Why do you hate flossing so much?"

"It's boring. There's nothing to do."

"A guy named Fritz Perls once described boredom as just a lack of attention. It's an interesting idea, don't you think?"

Dewey wasn't sure, but he was worried he was going to get bored hearing about it.

"It means, Mr. Dewey, if you're bored flossing it's not because flossing itself is boring. It's because you're doing a lousy job paying close attention to the quality of the experience."

Dewey rolled his eyes.

"Mom! Dad's giving me life lessons again!" he called out.

His dad laughed.

"You should think about it."

"Think about flossing?"

"Yes."

"Now?"

"No. Not now, son, next time you're flossing. Pay very close attention to your flossing next time you're flossing."

"You're insane."

"Fritz Perls, Dewey. Father of Gestalt psychology. I don't pull this stuff out of my—" His dad paused searching for the right word.

"Yeah?" Dewey smiled widely. "I'm paying attention."

His dad smiled back, kissed him on his head, and turned out the light.

"Night Dewey. I love you."

"Love you, too, Dad."

His covers felt heavy and warm and the sheets felt cool and crisp. Dewey felt too tired to even think and sank into a deep sleep.

Emoji Fun

"Listen to this bio," Dewey said as he leaned back in his office chair with his socked feet up on his desk. "Hi! I'm the mother of beautiful ninth and sixth graders—that also makes me the mother of last year's honor roll student, this year's volleyball star player, and our school's basketball point guard. When I'm not driving carpools or at work, my husband and I still like to hold hands and take a walk on the beach. #Momdaze, #rockstarkids #nevertoooldforlove."

"Holy moly guacamole! This is on her Facebook page, her Instagram, and . . . hold on, yup, same bio on her Twitter account, too."

"She's enthusiastic," Clara said.

"Oh, she's enthusiastic, alright. She's also totally clueless!" Dewey said, laughing hard now. "Look at this!"

Dewey got up out of his chair and showed Clara a picture of a text exchange Angelica had sent him.

Mom: :-] (Draw image here)

Angelica: what?

M: What do you mean what?

A: why did you send me a grimace?

M: That's not a grimace, that's a big smile!!!

"But wait! Oh, no. This is terrible, but it's so good! Look at this one!"

M: Grandma called this morning to say they had to take Molly to the vet. [Picture of cry-laughing emoji]

A: what's going on with Molly?

M: She's in a better world now.

"Oh, dear," Clara said. "Well, that's unfortunate."

"Unfortunate, but hilarious!" Dewey laughed so hard he had tears coming down his own face, just like the emoji. "Right. We need to solve the problem, of course.

Still!" He laughed again. "She texted about the dog dying and put the laughing emoji! Ha-ha!"

"Sir? Do you think it's because she can't see them? They are awfully small? Or do you think she can't figure out what they mean?"

"That's a good question. She likes her own posts. She writes her own status on someone else's wall. She thinks she's messaging privately and posts publicly. So, who knows. How can such a smart person suddenly sound so . . ." Dewey struggled for a word that wouldn't sound unkind.

"Dopey?"

"Okay, dopey."

"So where are you going to start?" Clara asked.

Dewey shrugged. "Stumped. I guess I should start by telling Archie I'm sorry his grandma's dog died."

Just then a text came in from Archie.

It was a selfie of him drenched.

```
A. just dumped a glass of water on my head.

hope you figure this out soon.

drying off to play on my 'puter tho so #stillworthit!
```

Dewey showed Clara the picture and text.

"Oh, dear. Well let's just let this one percolate, then, shall we?"

She patted him on the head and left him to "percolate," evidently not even planning to finish their conversation before Archie's text had interrupted them.

Break

"Want to come to my house for dinner?" Seraphina asked. "Elinor is having a sleepover. You guys can come hang out with us."

They were all sitting on a warm bench in the sun together during nutrition.

"When?" Dewey asked.

"Saturday. Wanna?"

"Yeah. I do."

"You *Dewey*," Colin laughed.

"Ha, ha. Can you?"

"Can I *Dewey* it Saturday? I think I can."

"Great! I'll ask my parents. What should we do?"

Dewey rolled his eyes in anticipation.

"What should we *Dewey*?" Colin corrected.

"OMG. Stop."

"Okay, okay. Let's figure something out, though, or Seraphina will have us out collecting rocks."

"You're a little testy today," she said.

"Nah. Hungry. Got anything?"

Dewey opened his backpack and pulled out a bag of sliced apples.

"Gimme."

Dewey reached in the bag and handed him a couple slices.

"Thanks."

"How about bowling?" Seraphina suggested.

"Yeah! Bowling. I haven't done that since Whatshisface's birthday party."

"Silas? That was hilarious!" Dewey laughed. "Remember how Lukas dropped the bowling ball right in the middle of his cake?"

"Seriously?!" Seraphina looked up and stopped twisting her hair mid-twist.

"His mom went insane!" Colin laughed. "They served us squashed cake."

"The bowling guy made Lukas wash the ball! Ah, that was great!"

"Okay, so we're not inviting Lukas," Seraphina said.

"What? No! He's hilarious!"

"Seriously?"

"Maybe. Could be fun?"

"Hmm. Maybe."

"Where's Elinor?" Colin asked.

The bell always rang so much faster than any of them expected.

"Not sure," Seraphina said standing up. "Text me later if your parents say yes."

"I know I can. I might need a ride. Dewbert?"

"Yeah, yeah. I'll ask."

MTDIGS

One of the things Dewey loved most about bowling were the shoes. He loved the way the leather soles glided along the floor, slippery and smooth until the flat rubber heel brought you to a stop. But before Dewey could kick off his shoes and slide his feet into someone else's rented ones, he had to figure out his game plan at Archie and Angelica's.

Their mom seemed to give so much weight to the articles she read. What if she found out that what she was doing wasn't good for kids? Or maybe herself?

Dewey did some searches online. "Annoying parents on Facebook." "Moms who annoy kids on social media." He found lots of information. Clearly, she wasn't the only one with this problem. Now all he had to do was get Archie and Angelica to read or talk about these articles where she could overhear them and see if that might help stop her.

Tomorrow was Friday. Hopefully, he could get some of this going before the weekend. He emailed the best articles to them both, along with the directions for them to read over them and both meet him at his office tomorrow after school.

The next evening at the Thomas' house, Angelica and Archie sat in the kitchen next to the family room where their mother was working on organizing some books on a shelf. Dinner was over, and Angelica had papers out on the kitchen table doing her homework while Archie sat at his laptop.

"I don't think she realizes that she's coming across like these other moms," Angelica said. "Do you think I should show her these articles?"

"No!" Archie said loudly.

"Sh! Not so loudly. She'll hear you," Angelica said.

Mrs. Thomas, of course, stopped her work and began to listen to her kids.

"Look, here's a test parents can take to see if they are annoying other parents. Should we take it for her?"

"Sure."

"Okay, you read."

"Do you brag?" Archie read from the parent survey on the article, 'Do You Annoy Other Parents on Social Media.'

"Yeah. She's gotta be."

"You make mistakes often because you don't understand social media?"

"Holy cow, yes!"

"Are you an over-tagger?"

"Hello!"

"Do you use Facebook when you should use Google to answer your search questions?"

"Oh YEAH she DOES! She JUST posted to her account the other day asking if anyone knew what day of the week Christmas would be this year."

Archie laughed.

"What about—"

Mrs. Thomas walked in with her hands on her hips.

"Do you kids have something you'd like to address with me?"

"Oh, Mom! What are you doing here?" Angelica feigned surprise.

"Please. I wasn't born yesterday. What's all this about?"

"What do you mean?" Archie asked, his cheeks coloring two shades redder than his hair.

"I mean, you two are all but yelling about me and acting like you don't want me to hear. What gives?"

"I can't take it! We've got this new family policy and suddenly you're all over my life!" Angelica burst out in tears again, just as she'd done in Dewey's office when they first met, and ran out of the kitchen.

Archie flashed his mom a big smile. None of this was in the plan they had gone over earlier this afternoon in Dewey's office.

She sighed.

"Oh, give me those," she said, reaching for the articles about annoying Internet parents and sitting down to read them.

"Fine. Fine. Okay," she mumbled as she read. Archie had gone back to his Minecraft game because although he felt worried about his sister being mad at him, with her out of the room he felt more concern about his base.

"Please. This isn't a problem. I was just trying to join in on the fun." She sighed again and put down the articles.

"Well, you can watch me if you want," Archie said, only too happy to show anyone who would watch all that he did in Minecraft.

She looked up and watched Archie quietly for a few minutes.

As she watched she got an idea, and grabbed her phone to look up "Minecraft basics."

"Arch," she said. "What resource do you wish you had more of?"

"Obsidian," he answered, not even wondering where she'd gotten that question from.

"Do you have a house?"

"I'm working on a sushi restaurant. Wanna see it?"

"Show me."

Archie went to his restaurant. It was near the ocean with a pathway leading to a wooden dock, a chest full of fishing rods nearby, and another chest to store the fish that were caught. The pathway leading from the ocean back to it was built out of cobblestone, dirt, and grass. Out front, a small wooden fence surrounded a koi fish pond. The restaurant had a big glass opening to the front with two iron doors that opened automatically when you stepped on the pressure plates. The walls were built out of quartz and the floor was made from wood. For the lighting, Archie used glowstone blocks recessed into the ceiling and right in the middle of the room, red stone lamps, fence, and trapdoors made a big chandelier. There were tables and chairs, and a long sushi counter built from concrete. Different colored glass window panes lined the walls.

"Wow! Can you show me how to do this?" she asked opening up her laptop.

"What do you want do to?"

"How do I start?"

"You need to pick your skin."

Archie showed her how to install the game and create a username.

A quick study, she figured something like "Archie's mom" wouldn't be all that popular, so she went with something that spoke to her, instead. "MTdigs. You know, like Mrs. Thomas Digs and empty digs because I'll be digging a lot of nothing for a while."

"Not bad!" Archie said, raising one eyebrow. "You want to turn on 'cheats?'"

"What's that? No! I don't want to cheat."

"It just helps when you're getting started," he said.

"Definitely, not."

Before he knew it, his mom had MTdigs up and running.

"Okay, well, you gotta make sure you survive the night so you need to chop down some trees, build a crafting table, and you need shelter.

"Mom," Angelica said. "I'm going to Pamela's now for a while. Okay?

Their mom, engrossed in all the tasks Archie just gave her, didn't look up.

"Mom. You hear me? Mom?"

"What, honey? Sure. Go ahead."

"Can I come back after dinner?"

"Sure."

"After eight?"

"Why not."

Angelica shot Archie a triumphant look and headed out the door.

Turned out that Archie's mom was pretty good at this, and found it a lot more interesting than social media. Archie wanted time to play games, but he didn't at all mind his mom doing it, too. In fact, it was kind of fun for him.

Dewey had cleared the path, and what Archie's mom uncovered was that when you're in survival mode with your kids, sometimes you gotta get creative.

The Return of the Ballbarian

“That’s a funny idea. Making something new look old,” Elinor said when the others introduced her to the newly remodeled retro-bowling alley.

“Well, if you call a hi-def video wall retro,” Dewey said.

The music pumped so loudly they could hardly hear themselves speak, and some movie Dewey didn’t recognize played behind the pins of each lane like flat screen TVs lined up in the Best Buy aisle.

Neon lighting split the bowling alley area in half like a pair of 3D glasses, the lanes and pins an underwater blue, the booth seats and wooden floor with the ball return machine magenta.

"Cool seat!" Colin said bouncing up and down and changing his shoes.

Seraphina's mom was nearby in a booth table where she could keep an eye on them. Every single one of her senses felt taxed. The dark lighting, neon blues and pinks with flashy neon signs of the bowling alley's name, and the fluorescent orange overhead lighting created a visual input virtually the same with her eyes open or closed. Up above the kids and to her immediate left was the arcade, a fully lit bright room, dinging, binging, clanging, and down below, the sound of pins crashing and people cheering. Cheap food—shrimp poppers, wings, pizza, and fries all hit her nose at once like a car pile-up on the 405 freeway. The table where she sat, hoping to escape into her book or her phone, felt sticky from the morning's syrup or jam, her seat hard and cold. She could think of no place on earth she'd hate more.

Down below, Dewey grabbed a ball, making sure the holes were the right size and the weight not too heavy. He did the moonwalk, sliding on the slick floor as the others laughed.

"Score sheet," Seraphina said, taking the lead to set it up. "Let's pick names for each other with the word ball in it.

"Dewey, I dub you 'Meatball!'" she said, laughing and typing it in.

"'Meatball?!"

"Pick a 'ball' name for someone else."

"I gotta think."

"Elinor, you're 'Eyeball,'" Colin said. They all laughed.

"Hairball," nodded Elinor to Seraphina. More laughter.

Seraphina typed it all in.

"I got it! Colin's 'ballerina.'"

"That's not a 'ball.' It's not 'ball-e-rina.'"

Seraphina laughed, typing it in as they saw it projected on the wall.

"You're up first, Meatball."

He rolled two gutter balls.

"Eyeball's up."

Elinor selected her ball, an orange one, and held it close to her chest, staring down the lane. She took a couple steps, swung her arm, released the ball and it rolled, knocking down six pins.

"Nice!"

"Whoa," Colin said. "Look at your hair!"

"What?" Elinor asked, trying to smooth it back into place as she balanced the heavy ball with one hand.

"The pink stripe in this light!"

"Oh! Hold, please," Elinor said, getting back in position. She rolled her second ball, knocking down one more pin.

"It's like, purple."

"I'd say more lilac," Seraphina said.

"Whatever it is, it's glowing. Cool."

Eyeball smiled.

The scoresheet read Hairball, and Seraphina took her turn, releasing the ball so gingerly it all but crept down the lane.

"Are you kidding?" Dewey laughed, confident the ball would stop before it even made it to the pins. The ball rolled along like an overweight pug on a walk.

Six pins went down.

Eyeball raised an eyebrow. "We're almost tied."

"How'd you do that with that absurd roll?" Dewey marveled.

Seraphina dried her hand on the little air vent and rolled another slow ball.

"No way! Spare!" Colin yelled. "Hairball!"

The screen lit up and did a light show celebration.

"Incredible," Dewey said.

Colin selected his ball, held it up to his chin, and stood at the dots on the floor eyeing the middle pin. Then, just when they expected him to release and roll, he pointed his left index finger on top of his head and began to twirl his entire body around his fingertip.

"Goofball!" They laughed.

"No. Not 'Goofball.' *That* would have been a fine name, thank you. You picked Ball-e-rina."

"True. Very true!"

Colin lined his pointed foot up on the center dot again and then dipped into a *plié,* followed by a tippy toe, tippy toe, up to the line before finally rolling and knocking down some pins.

They'd all laughed so hard they missed how many pins he'd knocked down and had to check the screen.

"It looks like you're up again, Ma'am," Dewey joked.

"Men can be ballerinas!" Seraphina objected.

"What about ball-e-rinas?" Elinor asked.

"Yes. YES! That, too?" Colin asked.

"Obviously," Seraphina said. "And you're still up."

"Right!"

Colin rolled again, this time straight to the gutter.

"*Tutu* many distractions?" Dewey laughed and they all joined him.

"Meatball's up again."

Eventually their thumbs began to get sore, and someone said 'Meatball's' name was making them hungry. So, Seraphina went to ask her mom if they could order some snacks. As they waited, Dewey sat on the big red vinyl lane side seating, taking in the smorgasbord of delights the room offered his senses. Was there anything better than the thunderous sound of the pins breaking? It made this satisfying clap, crack, like waves pulling off rocks at the beach.

He recognized the movie playing on the screens and it kept his attention, even though the sound wasn't playing. Music blasted and he could feel the bass vibrate under his seat and in his chest. The colors and the lights made it feel like night and a party even though it was day out, and the smells of people's food going by made his stomach gurgle with hunger. He wanted to eat it all.

"She say yes?" He asked when Seraphina came bouncing back.

"Yup. Whatever we want. Just asked us to add the cut-up veggie plate to whatever we order."

They polished off a little of everything and felt sluggish but good.

"'Nother round?" Colin asked, sucking some grease off his finger.

"Ha! You'll be Greaseball," Seraphina laughed.

"I'll take it!"

"I'll be Goofball," she said.

"That works," Dewey nodded. "I'll be Screwball."

"Definitely works." They laughed.

"Mothball."

"Mothball?" Dewey and Colin both said together.

"I don't know. It just came to me."

"Okay! Mothball it is!"

They got one more round of bowling going. This time, Seraphina and her slow-witted ball got a strike the third frame in.

"How is that possible?! Your ball barely moves!"

"I don't know," she genuinely reassured Dewey.

"I did really great last time I went bowling with my family," Dewey grumbled.

"You're up, Mothball."

Elinor lined her eyes up again with the arrow on the floor and her left foot with the dot before she swung and threw. She had power in her ball and knocked eight pins down.

She rolled again and got a spare.

"Okay. Well, *that* at least makes sense."

Seraphina and Elinor laughed.

Dewey was up and threw a good roll, knocking down five pins followed by three more. Greaseball fouled, stepping over the line his first frame. His second one he psyched himself up picturing himself on ABC Wide World of Sports. It was the big game. He was up for the league trophy. He tried to put a spin on the ball for a last second curve. He got a spare, but he wrenched his upper arm, his finger, and his thumb.

"I'm out!" he said. "Someone else finish for me."

Elinor sat on the red cushions drawing moths in her sketchbook. These were a different style from the manga she'd been working on earlier, more realistic. She liked the symmetry as she drew line segments on the wings, and feathered in texture and curves with a charcoal pencil. Each of the four petaled wings had a dark centered circle. They look like eyeballs, she thought, and smiled to herself about how their bowling names alighted on her page in more ways than one.

"We're almost done. Only two more frames left," Seraphina said.

"I can't," Colin said. "It's seriously throbbing."

"I can be done," Elinor said.

"To the end?" Dewey said to Seraphina.

"That's no fun, just the two of us. Lemme see if my mom will fill in for Colin. You'll still play, Elinor?"

"Sure," she said closing her sketchbook.

Seraphina came back with Mrs. Johnson.

"What size shoes do you wear, Colin?"

She borrowed his bowling shoes, which were a bit too small, but for two frames she wasn't renting a pair.

"Okay," Seraphina said. "You're Greaseball."

"Alrighty," she smiled

They began the line-up again, each taking their respective turns. Mrs. Johnson was up for Greaseball. She took a deep breath, wanting to be a good sport and rolled the ball. The gutter ball didn't shock her.

Her next roll bounced hard, not once, but twice, and then jumped into the lane of the people bowling next to them.

"Sorry!" she said, gesturing to them apologetically.

"Oh my—" Seraphina hid her face in Elinor's arm as the boys unsuccessfully tried to contain their laughter.

Elinor looked up from her drawing. "What'd I miss?"

"I guess it's been a while since I've played," Mrs. Johnson shrugged. "Looks like Goofball's turn."

But Seraphina couldn't go, because now the pins wouldn't clear since the ball hadn't gone down their own lane.

Dewey ran up to the counter to get some assistance.

"You can just buzz them," Colin said, pointing out the call button.

"I wouldn't know what to say," Seraphina said.

"Just tell them, 'my mom's a ballbarian.'"

Sibling Problem Solver

When Monday morning rolled in, Dewey had solved Archie's parent problem, not once, but twice. Archie had loads more freedom to play computer games, and Angelica wouldn't face more embarrassing TBTs or helpful articles on how to keep her room organized posted on social media.

And now, something else began to evolve in the biosphere.

Scientists believe that it wasn't until oxygen levels on earth reached a high enough concentration level that multicellular organisms like animals and plants began to evolve. So, it seems, it took just the mere presence of multiple kids in a family to grow the next facet of Dewey's career.

"Sir, this is different. Look at these three new requests."

Dewey had flopped down on the green cushion and never quite bothered to get up. Wolfie rested on his belly.

"This one says she has an annoying little sister," Clara read.

"Ha! Who doesn't!?"

Clara scrolled through their account, reading aloud highlights of what had landed in their inbox.

"Needs assistance with a tattle-tale brother . . . says his sister hogs the bathroom . . ." She continued to scroll. " . . . my brother ignores me . . . my sister locked me in plastic handcuffs and won't let me out . . . boss, these all came in over the weekend."

"I don't get it," Dewey sat up on the pillow, upsetting Wolfie's position. "These are brother-sister things." He pulled himself up to go look at them more closely.

"They most certainly are, sir."

"Do we do it?"

"Do what?"

"Take on a sibling case?"

"I presumed you already had."

"Huh?"

"Nothing, sir," Clara said, smiling and waving her remark away like a pesky fruit fly. "One interest you?"

"Lemme see those again," Dewey scrolled through. "Oh boy!" Dewey laughed. "I think we'd better start with Claire Bautista-Knickerbocker! Listen to this: 'I heard you're good at fixing sibling problems. My brother won't leave me alone. Yesterday he ran around with his fart in a jar chasing me. Can you help?!'"

"That sounds exigent," Clara said.

Dewey laughed. "Sure does! Um, what's that mean?"

"It means that it requires our attention."

"Right! Agreed. Claire's case first."

Dewey Fairchild, Sibling Problem Solver. That had a nice ring to it. Dewey thought about just how far he'd come since that first day when he and Seraphina had set out to solve her problem with her overprotective mother. She done pretty well, letting them bowl this past weekend without worrying they'd drop a ball on their foot or get held up by a bowling alley bandit. She could use some extra buttressing in the bowling skills department, Dewey thought, smiling. Dewey Fairchild, Uncoordinated-Mother-Problem-Solver? Who knew where he'd find himself next.

His musings came to an abrupt ending as none other than Pooh came careening down the office slide again, squealing with delight.

"Arf! Arf! Arf, arf, arf!" She ran around on all fours play-acting as a dog. Wolfie, usually quick to greet any new arrival, stood still on his own four legs staring at her.

"Sir?" Clara began.

"I see her, I see her."

"Allow me. Sit," Clara commanded showing Pooh a cookie like she was a real dog and Clara had a treat.

Wolfie sat. Dewey laughed and went to the fridge and snapped off a piece of carrot for him. "Here you go, Boy."

Clara dropped a cookie in Pooh's mouth and patted her on the head. "Good girl."

"Boy," Pooh corrected.

"Oh, pardon. Boy."

"Pooh. What are you doing here?" Dewey complained.

"Arf! Arf!"

Dewey rolled his eyes.

"Ugh!"

At that, she let out some small little noises that sounded a lot more to Dewey like air let out of the stretched mouth of a balloon than a dog whining, but he knew what she meant.

"Okay. Okay! You can stay. But go play with the real dog, will ya? We're doing work around here."

He didn't have time for her shenanigans. Cases were pouring in and he needed to prepare for Claire tomorrow.

Nothing

"Claire the pear wears green underwear.
Claire the pear wears green underwear.
Claire the pear wears green underwear.
Every day at night."

"Every day at night?!" Claire screamed at her brother. "What does that even mean?!" She said it to the trees, though. Maybe the mailboxes caught wind of it. Her brother had long taken off down the street on his bike. Why couldn't he just leave her alone? Adam Bautista-Knickerbocker was eighteen months younger than Claire, and just one school year behind. As she rode her bike home, she imagined ways she could make his life as miserable as he made hers. Maybe she would Super Glue his hands together and the only way he could text for help would be to use his nose or his toes. Maybe she should go directly to the problem and Super Glue his mouth, too!

When she reached her driveway, she hopped off and walked her seven-speed all-terrain mountain bike up the steep driveway. It had white handle bars, a hot pink frame, and black seat and tires. Her brother's bike lay on its side. She could hear him off in the bushes somewhere working on one of his homemade films. I hope he gets in trouble for just dropping it there, she thought. Maybe Dad will run it over.

Claire carefully leaned her bike against the side of the house and walked into its warmth. She could smell dinner cooking. During her meeting with Dewey earlier in the week, she had outlined all of the ways Adam tortured her. Today she and Dewey were capturing a-day-in-the-life by having her Facetime him every time Adam came near her.

"Even if he's not talking to you," Dewey had instructed, "just turn it on so I can see in case he does something. I'll be fine just weeding out moments when he doesn't do anything interesting."

"Well, you should be doing a lot of weeding out, then," she said sarcastically.

Claire had failed to Facetime Dewey when Adam 'Claired-the-Peared' her. Now she walked into the kitchen. She knew Adam was in the house, so she dialed Dewey just in case she ran into her brother again.

Claire saw Dewey on the screen. He gave her a thumbs up and she went about her business getting a snack in the kitchen. This time, of course, nothing.

She felt badly taking up Dewey's screen time for no reason.

The day went on with a whole lot more of nothing. Adam seemed to be out filming pill bugs under rocks or something, and Claire had no data to support her misery. Dewey texted her:

> new plan
>
> ill look at yr paperwork and plan a stakeout

She texted him back a thumbs up. Claire felt kind of gritty after her bike ride, so she went up to take a shower. She knew she shouldn't take such long ones, because California was in a drought. Everyone knew that, but once that hot water hit her back and the steam started filling up the room, it was hard to get out. For just a few minutes, Claire stayed in the hot shower to avoid thinking about the problems with her brother. The constant chatter of what happened yesterday or what might be happening tomorrow made way for the feeling of warm water, creamy soap, and her favorite, Mermoo, a fragrant green shampoo that smelled like jasmine and water lilies, layered with coconut and tropical beach.

"Wrap it up, Claire!" her mother knocked on the door.

So much for mermaid reverie.

"Okay," she called back, rinsing the shampoo from her long dark brown hair and watching the green lather run down the drain.

As she toweled dry, Claire looked up in the steamy mirror as big letters began to appear.

Adam had written CLAIRE STINKS across the mirror after he'd steamed up the bathroom from his last shower, and now they appeared, like invisible ink.

She quickly rubbed out the letters with her towel and then regretted she hadn't taken a picture of it for Dewey.

Ugh! Things were just not going her way. She sure hoped Dewey could help.

Slippery Kid

It had been a while since Dewey went on an undercover operation, unless you counted being in Archie's ear.

"This is gonna be fun! I have no idea where I'll hide. This is gonna be awful. Do you think I should bring snacks? I could get hungry. I love a good stakeout. I love a good steak. I have no idea what I'm doing. I—"

"Sir," Clara interrupted him. "I think you'll find much of what you need, other than the good steak, perhaps, in the paperwork Ms. Bautista-Knickerbocker filled out for us."

"Right. Paperwork. Right. Can you get—oh, thanks." Clara had already anticipated it, of course, and he found Claire's information pulled up on his computer screen as Clara gestured with her chin to lead him there.

"Let's see. Top three hiding places are her room, family room, and some play room. Okay. Entrance, front door. Hmm. That's a little tricky. Gotta figure that out. When do we think I should do this?"

"Oh," Clara said. "I just assumed tomorrow."

"Right. Tomorrow."

"Well, unless you want to spy on a weekday."

"Easier for me to get out of my house tomorrow. Tomorrow it is. How am I gonna eat?"

"Let's pack some rations today. PBJ for lunch?" she said, sticking her head in the cabinet. "Some sliced carrots. Cookies. You'll go home for dinner?"

"Yeah."

"I'm sure Ms. Claire can provide for you as well."

"Huh! It really has been a while! This should be fun. Unless I can't get in the front door. Or out. That'd be bad." He was all over the map again.

"It's like riding a bike, sir. Like riding a bike."

The next morning, Dewey told his parents he had a project with Claire. It was the time of day where the sun was out, but not hot overhead. The trees looked darker green right after breakfast, and the air still felt cool. As Dewey rode his bike over to her house, a sleepy shadow stretched out over the ground, and he crossed warm sunny patches along the way. He passed by Colin's, who lived only a few blocks away from Claire's, and wondered what he was doing now—still in bed? Eating a bowl of cereal? Dewey pulled up to Claire's driveway, and she met him outside.

Claire had on a gray ribbed turtleneck with the sleeves pushed up just below her elbows. She had long, dark hair that hung in soft waves long past her shoulders, halfway down her back. The tips of it danced a lighter brown from highlights that had long ago grown out to the very ends. A natural, hard-angled arch framed each of her deep brown eyes.

They tucked his bike and helmet into the bushes.

"All clear for me to come in?"

"Yeah. Adam's still in bed. My dad's out on a run, and my mom's cooking breakfast. Hide out in the family room, I think. Behind the big lounge chair's good. Right there, against that wall in the corner."

Dewey settled into his spot. Pretty roomy, he thought. He could lean his back on the wall and stretch his feet out and still not be seen. No pets. Bonus.

"What's she making for breakfast?"

"Pancakes. Want me to smuggle you one?"

Dewey flashed her a smile.

Like riding a bike, he thought.

It didn't take more than about ten minutes or so for Adam to come padding down in his Lego Star Wars BB8 pajamas. While it wasn't particularly apparent to Claire, Dewey noticed the family resemblance between the two of them right away. Adam stood about a head shorter than Claire, but had the same dark hair and eyes she did. He had his father's lighter skin and she her mother's darker tone, but otherwise, Dewey could have picked that kid out of a lineup as Claire's brother for sure.

In his right hand, he shook a can of Diet Coke that he'd been shaking for two weeks. The Bautista-Knickerbockers didn't usually have soda around, but a few weeks ago, his parents had some friends over for a BBQ, and they'd had some in a cooler. Adam swiped one and had been shaking it ever since, under the mistaken belief that the more days he shook it, the harder it would blow.

Usually, in the mornings, Adam's hair was smashed against his head more than Mario landing on a Goomba. This morning, while his face revealed the creases from his long night's face plant with his sheets, his hair was buried underneath not one, not two, but three knit winter hats.

"My hats!" Claire shrieked.

Adam shot her a look that said, 'come and get me if you dare.'

"You went in my room?!"

Claire grabbed the hats off his head and, kicking off

her slippers so they wouldn't slow her down, ran upstairs with them.

"Argh!" Dewey could hear her voice trail off on her way back into her room as she slammed her door.

Meanwhile, Adam, who now presumed he had the room to himself, shook the can some more and headed off into the kitchen. Dewey peered around the corner of the chair but ducked back when he heard Adam make his way back in again. Dewey saw him clutching two round pancakes in his fists. He took a bite of one from one hand, one from the other, and then shoved them both into Claire's slippers.

Whoa, Dewey thought.

Claire came back down and picked up where she left off with Adam.

"If you even think about going in my room again, I'll OH MY—WHAT THE—AHHHH!!!"

She pulled her feet out of the slippers and dug her fingers into them to pull out the smooshed pancakes.

"Are you serious? You want feet pancakes?! Here. Eat 'em." Just as she was about to shove them into Adam's face, Claire's dad came in through the front door back from his run.

"Dad!" Claire screeched clutching the pancakes in both fists, "Adam put—"

"Hey, there, pumpkin. Hold that thought, would ya?

I gotta take a quick rinse before breakfast is ready, otherwise when I cook tomorrow no telling how late mom will arrive to the table!"

"But—"

"Five minutes. Meet me at the pancake spot!"

"Argh!"

Adam laughed.

Dewey, still trying to recover from the fact that two perfectly golden delectable pancakes had been sacrificed to Claire's ten toes, typed tons of notes into his phone.

"Guys! Let's go! It'll get cold!" their mom called from the kitchen.

Dewey repositioned himself behind the arm of the couch. He couldn't catch much of a view other than their legs and feet under the table, but he could hear them.

The Bautista-Knickerbocker family enjoyed a hearty breakfast of pancakes, bacon, and fresh sliced farmer's market strawberries.

"So, what was it your brother did to vex you this morning, Claire?" her father asked, slicing a piece of sausage and pancake to place into his mouth together. He always chewed with his mouth closed.

Claire, mouth full of pancake, took a moment to chew and prepare to share her morning grievance. As she did so, however, Dewey noted something else at work. Adam shook his can of soda under the table. From his low vantage point, Dewey could see Adam tap Claire on her leg and then shake, shake, shake the can.

Claire seemed to get the message. Talk, and I'll blow this baby all over you.

She swallowed.

"Nothing. We worked it out."

"Now, that's what I like to hear," their mom said, smiling.

"Yes, indeed," their dad agreed. "Pass the pancakes, would you, please, son?"

"Sure, Dad. I'll slipper them right on over!" he said sliding the plate and flashing his sister a big grin.

After breakfast, they went upstairs to brush their teeth, Claire at her sink, and Adam at his own next to hers. She attempted to ignore him. As he brushed, the foam built up in his mouth and rather than spitting it into the sink, he let the buildup get wet and runny and drip down his arm until she could no longer stand it.

"That's disgusting." Claire spat into the sink and wiped her chin on the towel.

"What?" Adam said, standing there with the wet, drippy, runny toothpaste dripping down his forearm.

"Argh!" she stormed out.

Sticky Situation

After teeth were brushed and breakfast dishes done, the Bautista-Knickerbocker family headed out for a few hours. Adam had a soccer game and the family went to cheer him on.

"There are some leftovers in the fridge. You can heat them in the microwave," Claire offered Dewey. "I'm sorry we're leaving so long."

"No problem at all. Can I use your computer?"

Dewey made himself at home with a stack of pancakes, two slices of bacon and found an old Ren & Stimpy cartoon to watch on the computer. Then he checked in with Clara, began to flip through his notes a bit, texted Colin, and played some Minecraft until he got a text from

Claire saying they'd be back soon. She suggested he hide out next in her room, as she'd be doing some homework, and Adam would be upstairs since he needed to shower.

Dewey rinsed his plate and made sure the kitchen looked the same as he'd found it, albeit three pancakes and two bacons shorter, and headed up to Claire's closet.

As he opened Claire's closet door and moved some things around to make space, he spotted Claire's binders on her desk and considered how he might have brought some homework along for the downtime. He had five math problems to finish and had to start a chapter in a new independent reading book. Maybe he could just find a book to read in Claire's room. He stepped out of her closet to look at Claire's bookshelves to see if anything interested him. He found some he'd liked in fourth grade. What else? He pulled a book that looked like science fiction off the shelf, sat down on the white bedspread of her neatly made bed, and began to read.

Murder, mystery, outer space: he got lost in it within about forty-five seconds of reading, and forgot his place in the universe, let alone about the Bautista-Knickerbocker's return, until he heard the door open downstairs. Dewey jumped off Claire's bed and grabbed the book and got back into the closet to hide.

Claire came up to her room and plopped her stuff

down on her desk chair. Before Dewey could stick his head out for a friendly hello, Adam was hot on her heels.

"Stop it!" she yelled.

"Three, two . . ." Adam counted down, shaking and threatening to open the soda can.

"Mom!!" Claire yelled, running out of the room as he chased her.

"In the yard, Claire."

Claire ran from Adam as he chased her like a mad bee at a picnic. She ran back into her room and tried to slam her bedroom door, but he pushed it open and in he came.

"One!" He pulled the tab. From inside the closet, Dewey heard the pressurized can's explosion and Claire's scream as the sound of soda spraying hard and fast hit the air.

"Uh oh," Adam said.

Diet cola had sprayed all over Claire's bedspread, walls, and dripped from the ceiling down onto the carpet. Wow. How could there be so much liquid in one small can, Dewey wondered, peering out through a crack in the closet door.

"Uh, oh," Adam said again, paralyzed as the cola dripped down onto his head in large drops. He also wondered how such a small can could produce so much liquid. It was better than he'd ever imagined. And worse.

Claire's face, chest, and arms dripped in sticky wet cola. She stood frozen, stunned, like a statue in the rain, her hair wet with droplets of soda, her eyes crying drops of diet cola tears.

Adam slowly walked backward out of the room, reached the doorknob with his back toward the door, and fumbled with the door behind him, never taking his eyes off Claire. He wasn't sure what she might do to him, but he was pretty sure he'd gone too far and he wasn't sticking around to find out.

Dewey slowly opened the door to Claire's closet and looked at her.

"Borrow this?" he asked, gingerly holding up the book.

She nodded ever so slightly so as not to shake any extra drops off her wet self.

"I'll just let myself out. I'd say I've got enough data. Yup. P-lenty. We'll talk tomorrow. Tonight maybe."

Claire just stood there, getting stickier by the moment, and offered another almost indiscernible nod and licked her lips.

"Okay, then." Dewey could find no good closure. No easy exit. He couldn't very well offer to help her clean it up and risk getting caught. Leaving her in that mess was cruel! He handed her a tissue, and then another. Then, he carefully placed his hand on her damp shoulder.

"You're in a sticky situation, alright," he nodded slowly as she just stared at him.

"Don't worry. I'll figure it out." He kept nodding on his way out, more to convince himself than Claire. "Thanks for the book?"

He thought teacher problems were hard? He should have known! Sibling problems would be a nightmare!

The Big Reveal

Dewey remembered the day his baby sister was born. They had all talked about what would happen that special day—how Clara would come babysit, and how his parents would go to the hospital to have the baby.

Still, when he came into the kitchen and found Clara and not his mother or father, Dewey still remembered how his small heart jumped.

"They're at the hospital," Stephanie said, eating a bowl of cereal.

Clara sat down and patted her lap for Dewey to hop up.

"The baby is on her way!" she added. "You'll get to meet her soon."

Dewey had wanted a baby brother, not another sister. He already had a sister. He wanted a boy. But, he did feel excited to meet any baby now. He and his mom had decorated the baby's room with some of his paintings. They had a list of names, and he got to peek when no one else did. He wondered which name they would pick.

"When can we go?" he asked jumping off Clara's lap and then up and down.

"As soon as we get the call."

Dewey remembered that day staying home and baking cookies with Clara. Little did he know, six years later, those same warm cookies and that very same Clara would be sitting with him on a comfy couch together in their small attic office, learning about kids and new siblings.

"What a disaster!"

Kid after kid had parent after parent thinking it was fun to surprise them with the big reveal news. Kids popped balloons filled with either pink or blue confetti. Kids bit into cupcakes with pink or blue frosting to reveal what 'flavor' their new baby would be.

But in YouTube video after video, the big reveal Clara and Dewey witnessed on their big screen was that the kids didn't think that this was a fun game at all!

"I don't want to pop it!" What little kid would? Well, Dewey would, but he got why that little guy was afraid. It was a big fat balloon and was going to make a big fat noise, and little kids like to hang onto their balloons. Everybody knows that, Dewey thought.

Dewey and Clara watched as the mom in the video tried to pop it for the little guy.

She went to grab the balloon, but her big pregnant belly wouldn't let her reach it. She bumped it by mistake with her belly and it floated to the floor, at which point she tried to bend and pick it up, but no luck there either. She was coaxing her son to pick it up. Finally, the camera dipped and Clara and Dewey were watching their ceiling as her husband got the balloon and a pencil and handed them to the kid.

Finally, the kid closed his eyes, stuck in the pencil tip, and out shot pink confetti. "So!" the parents coaxed the kid. "What do you say! You're going to have a baby *sister!*"

Dewey watched as the kid dropped his head like an anvil.

"I don't want a baby. I want a balloon!" he cried, stomping his foot. "Waah!!" he wailed and wailed.

"What a bust," Dewey laughed at his own play on words. "Get it? Bust?"

"Got it, sir."

"Wonder how that all worked out?" Dewey stuffed some popcorn into his mouth.

Next came the kid with the gender reveal cupcake.

"Okay, Mommy and Daddy have a surprise for you today! We have a cupcake for you! If it's blue inside it's a boy, and if it's pink inside, it's a girl!

She just ate her little cuppie cake, happy as can be, when wham. She hit the blue center.

"Oh, nooo! I want pinkkk!" she was crying. "I want pink! No fair!!"

"But it's not a girl. It's a boy. You're going to have a little brother," they explained.

That little kid in a pink top, with a picture of a pink scientist bear on it with a pink bow and pink and purple beakers, folded her arms across her little chest and wailed with her blue tongue, "Give him back!"

"These are funny," Dewey laughed. "But they're awful! And look at these pictures of when the babies come home. Do these siblings look happy?!"

Dewey flipped through a bunch of pictures of babies being held by older siblings. One girl frowned so much Dewey laughed, commenting on how he thought people only *drew* sad mouths turned down that much. Another boy looked as if he'd flush that baby down the toilet, given the chance. These were some funny pictures, and some unhappy siblings.

"Wonder how it went when they told Claire about the new baby and brought him home? They're only eighteen months apart. But wouldn't it make more sense, then, that she'd torture him, not the other way around?

"I don't remember anything from eighteen months. Claire's not gonna either. She'll have to ask some questions. There's got to be something to all of this that can help me figure out how to help her."

"Eighteen months apart, you say? I do have one thought, sir."

Dewey looked up hopeful and nodded her on.

"Baboons don't laugh at each other's bottoms."

If there was one thing Dewey had learned, it was that when he had no idea what Clara was talking about, help was on the way.

"Baboons? Bottoms?"

"Ever seen one?"

"Maybe at the zoo? They have those big long faces?"

"Right," she said, pulling up an image.

"That's what I thought," he said, looking at the picture. "And they have those big red puffy butts!" Dewey laughed. "I love those!"

"That's right. Shaggy all over. Except, sir, their faces. And their rather pronounced bottoms."

"Ah," Dewey nodded, still not understanding why in the world they were talking about baboons and their bottoms.

"Adam and Claire, you've said, are close in age. Perhaps a common cause," she said, smoothing her already smooth gray bun.

Dewey didn't dare interrupt with a question.

He looked at her, hardly daring to blink.

She looked back at him, smiling gently.

"Alrighty, then," she slapped her knees and stood up.

"What? Huh?"

She looked at him, waiting for him to continue.

He looked at her, waiting for the same.

"The baboons? Their bottoms? I don't get it."

"The saying?" she asked.

"I guess so?" If she didn't know, he knew he sure didn't.

"Oh, it's an old idiom. Perhaps two peas who find themselves in the same pod might feel sympathy toward one another if the circumstances warrant it."

Now she had introduced peas in a pod. She was layering idiom atop idiom.

Peas. Pods. Baboons. Bottoms. Hang on, thought Dewey. I can get this.

"You mean the baboons don't laugh at each other's ridiculous butts because they're in it together?"

"Precisely." She gave one nod of her head.

"Okay!" Dewey clapped his hands together. "But Claire and Adam aren't in it together."

"Not yet."

"Oh," Dewey drew out the word, and as he did so, his mouth formed the same round "o" as that very small word he had just made very long.

Heads Up, Dewey

The plan seemed simple enough. Dewey had to get Adam and Claire to have a united cause. Five minutes into thinking about it, Dewey was already smacking his own forehead. Simple enough? What was he thinking? Simple would be getting Seraphina excited about flying mini-drones and Colin out there collecting rocks. Adam's last stunt was going to make this a humongous task.

Dewey spent the morning trying to come up with what they could possibly have as a common plight, given that they were not both sitting on red swollen bottoms. Nothing came to him though.

"I'm hungry," he grumbled. "My legs hurt from sitting in this chair for so long." He got himself a snack and played a few rounds of Clash of Clans to clear his mind. Then, he went online to see what he could find on the topic of helping siblings to get along.

"Ha! Make them hold hands until they're friendly again?! I don't think so!" he laughed, shoving a pretzel into his mouth. This was a funny idea—t-shirts sewn together trapping siblings to make them figure out how to get along.

"Haha! If all else fails," Dewey laughed. "I wonder if they have three-headed ones? I can just see me, Pooh, and Steph all crammed in one of those! Money jars for each fight. Lots of talking about feeeeelings. Share something positive at the dinner table." What, like, 'I'm positive this can of soda is going to explode all over you?', Dewey thought to himself.

Nothing he read seemed quite right. These all worked with what they *didn't* have in common.

Maybe I'm going about this the wrong way. I gotta figure out something that gets Adam to put all of his torture talents into defending Claire instead of tormenting her. Good, Dewey thought. Good! Hmm. What did they share in common that he might want to defend her about?

He texted Claire and asked her to send him a list of everything she could think of that she and Adam had in common.

```
everything food games people hobbies
whatever you can think of
```

Dewey also decided as bitter a pill it would be for Claire to swallow, he actually liked the idea of sharing one positive thing at the dinner table. It might prime Adam's pump if Claire said something nice about him. Dewey would tell Claire to suggest the idea to her parents as something they learned in health class. Whose parents wouldn't go for that? That's just the kind of thing parents eat up at dinner, he chuckled to himself.

Phew. Things were sort of moving in the right direction. He'd wait for the list back from Claire and then feed her the dinner conversation suggestion.

"Get it, Clara? See what I did there? 'Feed her the dinner table conversation.'"

Clara's eyes crinkled in a smile.

After Dewey had finished all of this problem solving and catching Clara up, he felt he needed to catch up with his friends. He wondered if Elinor and Seraphina would have another sleepover this weekend. Colin and Dewey wanted to figure out how to use their mini quadcopters to take pictures instead of just flying it around. He texted Colin a GIF of a mini-quad hovering. Colin returned one with an owl doing the identical kind of hover. Dewey then sent a cat trying to bat around and catch a mini-quad flying over a bed, and Colin sent a GIF of a rat flying, a mini-quad attached to its head and tail. Dewey laughed.

`when we go out?`

`tomorrow`

When Dewey got to Colin's he realized he'd forgotten to bring extra propellers.

"Do you have any?"

"Yeah, pretty sure."

But he didn't.

"We'd better go out on the grass, then."

They rode their bikes to the open elementary school field.

"I remembered the memory card, though," Colin said, sliding it into his mini-drone.

"You know my dad says the military uses these to study how animals do stuff so they can imitate them?"

"I know, right? Cool."

"Yeah. They figure if they can learn how to fly like a bat or swim like a fish or whatever, then they'll have one leg up."

"Or a fin."

Dewey rolled his eyes.

"They're also trying to make these things as small as bugs."

"I think they already have."

"So cool."

"Okay, so what do we wanna do?"

"Some selfies and overheads. Maybe some stills of those buildings?"

Dewey began to lift his mini-quad off the ground, but it just hovered and crashed back down on the grass.

"Maybe some flying practice?" Colin laughed.

"I'm rusty," Dewey said flatly as he blew grass blades off his drone.

Colin set his 'copter down and did some warm-up tricks.

"Why don't we just try with mine to start so we can save the battery in the other one?"

Dewey agreed and they set off to find something they'd want to film.

"Climb the tree. I'll fly it up and take pictures," Colin said.

Dewey looked around to make sure no one would object, handed Colin his mini-quad, and shimmied up the tree.

A cool breeze blew on his face, and his hands felt a bit raw from his quick ascension.

He looked down at Colin, who began to send the humming mini-quad up.

"Make a face. Do something."

Dewey slid himself out a bit more on the limb and wrapped his legs tightly around the thick branch. Grabbing on with his hands, he swung his body so he hung upside down. Out dropped his phone and some loose change.

"Oh! Good! Stay there!" Colin yelled from below. He lowered the drone until it hovered just in front of Dewey's face. As the blood rushed to Dewey's head his tongue began to feel heavy in his mouth, and his ears got full like they were underwater. He felt his upper cheek bones thicken as if someone drew them in with heavy black lines and a slight headache loomed in the background. This was fun! He wondered how it was turning out.

"Okay, that's it!" he groaned and laughed as he pulled himself up, the drone still hovering and filming.

"That was great!"

Dewey climbed back down and felt the blood run back to his face as the laws of nature righted themselves in his body.

"Did we get anything good?"

Dewey picked up the change and his phone. Phew. No cracks. But there was a text. It was from Claire. She had sent her list of things in common with her brother. Dewey couldn't believe what he read.

Dewey's Got Visitors

Claire's list read as follows:

Both want a dog but can't have one

Both like ice cream, different kinds

Sometimes make up funny songs together

Like the beach

Like spaghetti

Like tacos

Like strawberries

Like Uncle Kenny

Hate cauliflower

Hate tomatoes

Love bike riding

Don't like long car trips

Don't like emptying dishwasher

All this drama and nothing exciting on this list at all. How was that possible, Dewey wondered? How was this going to come together? Well, Dewey thought. Bikes. Bikes seemed like as good a place as any. She had one. He had one. Adam had one. He could figure something out with bikes. He sat tossing his phone up and down in his hand that way his dad hated as he thought his way through the alphabet rhyming with bike to see if anything hit him as an idea of what to do with the bike. It was as good an approach as any.

Bike. Fight. Maybe, something with the bike and a fight? He'd come back to that. Hike. Like. Mike. Pike. Psych. Psych. That could work. How could they psych him with the bike? Tell him someone stole it? That could work Dewey thought. That's good. That's good-ish, anyway.

Dewey sat at his desk. The late morning sun filtered through the window on the other side of the room, so he had the light on his desk turned on. Clara wasn't in, and he had the office to himself. There were no cookies out. It was quiet—only the hum of the refrigerator filled the air. Dewey opened a picture of a bike online somehow thinking this might inspire him to fill in the details of the operation whose details remained fuzzy.

Just at that moment, the tell-tale sounds of someone crawling into the vents could be heard followed by the thump and arrival of a guest. As his brain tried to make sense of the visual message his eyes sent it, Dewey's heart jumped and he found himself back in that place where perception gets jumbled by expectations. He simply could not compute that Stephanie sat on his green client pillow. Not as challenging to decipher was what abruptly followed—the rough landing of Pooh Bear.

"See?!"

"Whoa."

"See?!" Pooh repeated, standing up. "Where's Wolfie?"

Dewey could not even find his tongue let alone form words.

Stephanie began walking around.

Dewey found his voice.

"Stop. You're not supposed to be here."

"And you are?"

He threw up his hands.

"See?!"

"Stop saying that!" Dewey yelled.

"What?" Pooh asked, confused.

"Go!"

"What? No way. What is all this? Spill!"

"It's nothing. It's nothing. You're not here. This isn't happening. I'm not the most miserable person in the world right now." He pushed them both onto the Gator as he spoke and pushed the button to lift them up.

"Dewey! What is all of this! I want to—"

"Off you go," Dewey cried out.

He slumped into his chair and texted Clara.

```
sos

sisters onslaught surprise
```

Bruno

Colin had some very funny pictures of Dewey hanging upside-down from the tree.

"Pretty good!" Dewey said, chomping on a chocolate brownie snack bar. "What should we do with them?"

"Maybe the Pentagon wants them to study weird insects."

"Weird insects . . ." said Dewey, Googling the topic in his phone. "Whoa, look at these. This one looks like a leaf!" he said, holding up his phone so Colin could see.

"What do they call it?"

"Giant Leaf Insect," Dewey laughed. "Oh, this's the one I'm gonna to be! Assassin bugs inject deadly saliva into their prey and then suck out all of the guts and stuff.

That totally sounds like one the Pentagon would want to study."

"Well, you look more like a monkey than a bug in these," Colin said, holding up a shot from the drone of Dewey dangling upside down. "These're pretty good, but we gotta get better at fly-by shots and reveals. After school?"

"Nooo. I've got a whole mess on my hands. I've got this case I'm working on. Plus, I didn't tell you! Pooh brought Stephanie up to the office. Now they both know about it."

"Really? Now what?"

Before Dewey could answer, which was just fine since he had no answer, Seraphina and Elinor showed up with their snacks and joined them on the grassy area where the students gathered.

"Damp?" Elinor asked putting her hand to the ground.

"No," Dewey answered. How come everybody else thought about that first?

Seraphina put down her sweatshirt on the ground first anyway.

Colin showed the pictures of Dewey.

"Nice! How'd you get a closeup shot from that height?"

"Mini-drone."

"I saw one of those you can control with your phone," Elinor said. The bell rang before they could talk more.

Why were these breaks so short? Dewey thought. Just enough time to start a conversation before they had to end.

After school, Dewey walked over to Claire's house.

"Here's the plan. I'm going to ride your bike home and stash it at my house. You're going to discover it gone and cry your eyes out. Get him to feel sorry for you and want to help you find it. Meanwhile, I'm going to work it on my end to make sure he's good and invested. Just play along."

"Hope this works," Claire sighed, sliding her hands in the back pocket of her jeans.

"It'll work. Did you do your 'gratefuls' at dinner?"

"Yeah, I told him I was grateful he makes me laugh, just like you told me. I wanted to barf."

Claire motioned Dewey to the side of the house where her bike leaned against the wall.

Dewey laughed. "It's a little pinker than I'd counted on riding down the street. Maybe we can take off this basket?"

"No. I love that basket!" The front handle bars held a brown wicker basket attached by two Velcro lined leather straps. "It's Amish."

Dewey laughed when he looked inside. "You have a dog in there!" He pulled out a stuffed tan puppy dog. It had little Cs for ears, a high-hung apostrophe tail, a black button nose, and two small round eyes, brown, with black puddle pupils.

How, wondered Dewey, could a little stuffed animal be so expressive?

"It's my Lhasa Apso, Bruno. Our parents won't let us have a real one."

"This is good. This is great! Okay. I'll keep the basket. He's coming with me."

"Really?" Claire's voice squeaked.

"Don't you see? It's even better than I thought. I'll work in the Asa Lapso, too."

"Lhasa Apso."

"Right. Lapso Apsa."

Claire giggled.

"Anyway, leave it to me. I'll take good care of little Bruno."

"Can't I just hide him in my closet? He won't find him."

"You gotta trust me, Claire. He'll be fine. You have my word. He's potty trained, right?"

She rolled her eyes.

"Right! So, we're all good!" Dewey hopped on her bike and looked over his shoulder to make sure no one was around to see him. "I'll be in touch soon."

Claire leaned into the basket and gave Bruno a kiss goodbye and pat him on the head.

"Go find him and let him know about your bike. And try to keep it just between the two of you. You need him to solve this with you, not a bunch of grown-ups. That'll be a whole other mess."

"Good thing I'm not the one who leaves my bike in the driveway all the time. They'd notice his missing in a heartbeat."

Dewey gave a final glance over his shoulder and strapped her helmet to his head. He had not thought to bring his own. Now, Dewey Fairchild rode off down the street on Claire's pink bike with the Amish basket, wearing her purple, pink and light blue splatter helmet covered with shooting stars. Dewey thanked the heavens above no one saw him.

Black Light, Brown Bag

As soon as Dewey left, Claire set off to do her part. She went to the bathroom and tried standing in front of the mirror to see if she could get her eyes to squeeze out any fake tears. She stared at herself, her long brown hair and brown eyes looking back at her, but nothing came. She could still see the remnants of the message Adam had left for her in the mirror—AIR STINK it read now, as the CL and final E and S had smudged off when she wiped it earlier. That made her laugh. It's funny to watch yourself smile for real in the mirror, she thought. It looks different from smiling fake for a camera.

She wet her fingertips with a few drops of water from the faucet to wipe Adam's message off the face of the earth for good when she got her idea. She could use the water from the faucet to make fake tears. She tried dropping a few right under her eyes and inspected. Nice! But how could she get them on demand for the moment required?

She looked around the bathroom drawers and cabinet for an eye or ear dropper but found only one that had swimmer's ear drops in them, and she was pretty sure she'd be in trouble if she dumped that out.

She found an ointment in a sandwich-sized re-closable bag. That will work, she thought, remembering how they'd filled those baggies with icing at Christmas to decorate the holiday cookies. She could fill one with water, poke a pin-sized hole in the corner and drop tear-sized water down her cheeks!

She headed into the kitchen to set it up, and just in time, because Adam came ricocheting in to get a snack. Claire sat at the round kitchen table. The walls of the sitting area were white, and the kitchen had cream tiles. Five long open shelves with plates, cookbooks, pitchers, mugs, and a couple of leafy green plants lined the wall. The Bautista-Knickerbocker family had painted one wall with green chalkboard magnetic paint, and on it was the week's events, some grocery items, some stick figures and hearts, and a magnet holding a dish towel. A small prep island separated the table from the kitchen where Adam stuck his head into the refrigerator.

Claire, without anything sharp to poke a corner in her water bag, bent down and rubbed her top and bottom front two teeth quickly together until just the tiniest of openings allowed water to seep out. With Adam still rummaging around in the fridge, she carefully squeezed a drop or two under each eye, tipped the bag the other way in her lap so it wouldn't leak, and put her head down in her arms.

"Sniff, sniff," she began when she heard him shut the fridge door. She added some shaking of her shoulders for effect.

"Claire?"

"Sniff, sniff," and she added a little hiccup sound.

"Claire?" he repeated. "What's wrong?" He hadn't caused the suffering, so he concluded it could actually be serious. Adam sat down next to her.

Claire lifted her head and he saw her tearful face. "Someone took my bike," she sobbed.

"Gone?! You sure?"

"Yes! It's gone!" she wailed and put her face back into her crooked arm on the table. "Go see for yourself."

Adam went outside to check, giving Claire time to add more droplets to her face and dump the bag in the sink.

"You're right! When did this happen?"

"I don't know, I don't know!" she began to pace.

"Don't worry, Claire," he said reassuringly, reaching up to pat her shoulder. "We'll find it." Adam looked around and couldn't find any tissue. He went to the bathroom and came back, trailing a long piece of toilet paper to give her to wipe her eyes and blow her nose.

Claire had to try hard not to laugh. She felt something that resembled warmth in her chest at the sight of him trying to help her. She felt half bad. Almost.

The next day, Dewey put phase two of the plan into effect by leaving Claire a ransom note. He took letters from a magazine, cut them up, and glued them onto a piece of paper. He rolled the letter up, stuck it in Bruno's collar, and left them both on the porch. The note read: 'We have your bike.'

"Claire! Claire! They really *do* have your bike! They left Bruno as proof! They've made contact!" Adam cried as he held the letter up to the light as if that might somehow reveal more about its authors. Claire felt grateful Dewey had returned Bruno. Now what, she wondered. She needn't have wondered long, for as Adam held up the letter, he realized there was more to it.

"Wait. I think there's more here, Claire," Adam said. "Go get me a black light."

"A black light? I don't have a *black* light."

"I'm telling you, there's more here."

"Where are you getting a black light from?"

"You can get them anywhere. Amazon. Hardware store."

"No, I mean, where are you getting that we *need* one from?"

"Right here," he said, holding up the ransom note. "Here's your dog *black*," he read.

"Oh. I didn't even notice that," she said.

"Well, I did."

"Don't you think it's just a typo?"

"A typo?!" Adam threw his arms up in the air in complete exasperation. "Claire, they are cut out letters."

"Good point."

"Okay, I'll go ride—"

"You were going to say you'd go ride your bike down to Busy Bees weren't you?" he said, gently reaching up and putting his hand on her shoulder again. "You can take my bike."

"Thanks," she said, feigning feeling all glum. She didn't have to feign feeling curious about that note, though. Even though she knew its author, she really did start to wonder what they might uncover.

Bring a brown paper bag filled with tootsie pops to the bridge by the elementary school. Leave it at the foot of the bridge by 3:00. Wait for further instructions.

That's what the note said when they shined the black light on it.

"Okay! We know their demands! We just have to bring the loot to the bridge."

The whole thing seemed absurd to Claire. She couldn't believe Adam was falling for any of it. "I don't even get how you knew to shine the black light," she said.

"It was obvious. I told you. No one leaves a ransom note with a typo."

"That's true. No one does."

"Okay!" he began again. "I'll go to Pal's and get the tootsie rolls and we'll do it. Don't *worry* so much, Claire. We'll get your bike. I promise."

Claire wasn't worried, of course, about her bike. She was worried this whole thing was somehow going to blow up like the center of the tootsie pop in her face. But she was in too deep now. She sighed.

"Thanks," she said.

Pal's was the name they gave to the corner mini-mart down the end of the block. It wasn't really called that, but Pal was the owner's name, and the kids in the neighborhood all called it that. Gone were the days of the mini-mart filling up a plastic bag for you in California. Adam was proud of himself that he remembered to bring a reusable bag with him, the contents of which he now dumped onto Claire's bed.

"I couldn't decide if I should just get a few flavors or a bunch of different kinds. So I got two of each," he said, lining up the Tootsie Pops as pairs on her comforter like dance partners. "Chocolate, cherry, orange, grape, raspberry, pomegranate, strawberry-watermelon, and lemon, which is disgusting, but I guess some people like citrus in their candy."

"Orange is citrus."

"Yeah, that's gross, too."

"Did you get extra?" she asked, going for a chocolate one.

"No!"

We can just take that pair of chocolate out." She handed them each one, smiling.

"Okay," he said, pulling off the paper and popping it into his mouth. The flavor of hot cocoa mingled with the feel of hard plastic on his tongue. "Sure hope this doesn't make or break the deal. What if bike-nappers like chocolate best?"

"Hmm," Claire said, her cheek round with a bulge from the lollipop. "Probably okay, but maybe we can get a few more to fill the bag a bit more." She punctuated the end of the sentence with the snap it made against her tongue and lips as she pulled the lollipop out.

"What time is it? After noon! We'd better get going!"

Pothole

Little did Dewey know, Claire and Adam had hit a pothole along the way.

"How long has it been missing?" Their dad asked, holding the ransom letter in his hand. His brow lowered and his lips pressed together closely into a thin line.

Claire gulped hard. Adam replied. "Day before yesterday?"

Adam told his dad all about the bike missing and the ransom letter.

"I appreciate, Adam, that you wanted to help your sister, but this is a job for the police, and someone should have told your mom and me."

"But Dad," Claire said, finding her voice. "It's obviously a kid and just a joke or a game."

"Stealing property isn't a game. This is an opportunity for you kids to learn how to report a crime."

He's going to make this a teachable moment. And he's mad. We're doomed, thought Claire. There's no stopping that train once it's headed down the tracks. This time it was headed straight for the police station. Her heart began to beat fast, and her palms felt sweaty as they rested against her legs.

"Are you going to call 911?" Adam asked excitedly.

"We call their non-emergency number," he said, pointing to a number written on the chalkboard wall. "It's always right there next to where it says 911, see? You're going to make the call, Claire."

"What, no!" Her face reddened.

"I'll teach you how and what to say."

"No. Dad. Noo!"

"You say, 'Hi. I'm Claire Bautista-Knickerbocker. I'd like to report a stolen bike.' Then they'll ask you questions and you answer them. I'll be right by your side."

Adam clapped his hands together. "Can I do it? Can I do it?!"

"I think since it's Claire's bike we should let her."

"Ugh. Dad! Can we wait a couple days and just see if it turns up?"

"No, sweetie. These things have to be handled right away."

Claire began to call the number and then stopped.

"Can I at least go to the bathroom first?"

"By all means."

As she walked away, she looked at Adam and motioned for him to follow her.

He shrugged at her, indicating a sort of 'what do you want?' look.

When he didn't follow, she motioned more frantically, so he followed.

"What?" Her red-alert level seemed disproportionate to the circumstances.

She pulled him into the bathroom and closed the door.

"Oh no. Oh no. This is bad. This is bad." She paced in the small space of the bathroom floor.

"What?" he repeated.

"You can't tell Dad."

"What?" He really thought she was making a big deal over nothing. He'd be glad to call the police.

"Promise you won't tell."

"Won't tell what?"

"Adam!"

"Yes. Promise. What?"

"My bike wasn't stolen. I, er, gave it to a friend."

Keep Your Eye on the Ball

"You gave it away?"

"Shhh! Not so loud. Not away. Just to . . . borrow."

"Why'd you tell me it was taken? We got that letter. You're not making any sense."

Downstairs, they could hear the doorbell ring and Mr. Knickerbocker talking at the door.

"Claire, Adam. Come on down, would you? I have a situation at work. I'm going to have to go handle it. We'll deal with your bike when I get back."

Claire began to cry real tears, whether from relief that she'd gotten a momentary reprieve or from panic, she wasn't sure herself, only that they wouldn't stop flowing.

"Okay, Dad," Adam called down. They heard the door close after him.

"Come on," Claire said, wiping her tears with the back of her hand.

"Where?" Adam asked.

"No more questions. Just come on."

They slid one after the other like a pair of penguins down a hill into Dewey's office. Adam looked around, totally amazed. He used the tip of his tongue to get the remaining cookie out of his back molars.

"What is all this?" he asked, looking around as his eyes took in as much information as he could. One piece of vital information had just become clear. Claire's bike leaned up against the wall.

Dewey, who wasn't expecting Claire, let alone Adam, stood up to greet them.

"Hey, Claire. What's up?" He looked to her to fill in the blanks.

"Oh, Dewey. It's all messed up. As soon as my dad gets home from work he's making us call the police to report my bike stolen."

Stolen. Well, this was an unexpected development.

"Sit down, you two," Dewey offered Adam a seat and dragged Clara's over for Claire. Clara, of course, wasn't in since it was Sunday. In fact, it was only by chance that

Dewey had been in the office himself. He'd come in to try and figure out what to do about this whole Stephanie/ Pooh Bear problem. He felt maybe if he stood there and stared at the space, it might somehow inspire him with a way to ensure they didn't ruin his entire operation.

He went to the freezer to pull out some cookies and put them on a plate.

"Oh, there were some along the way," Claire reassured.

"That's Clara. Always ready. Here. These are a bit chilled, but give them a minute or two."

Adam didn't wait. Nothing wrong with a frozen cookie in his book.

Dewey sat back down. "Catch me up."

"Catch *me* up," Adam said, munching on the cookie by putting it to the back outside of his teeth where he could bite down on its hard surface.

Claire looked at Dewey. Dewey looked at Adam. Adam looked at Claire who looked back at Dewey.

"Ugh. Let me catch Dewey up first, Adam. It was going fine. Great, actually, until my dad saw your note and then he w—"

"'Your note?'"

"That's right," Dewey nodded.

"And now he wants me to call the police! The POLICE, Dewey!"

"Yes. I agree. This isn't good. Lemme think."

"Could someone please explain to me what is going on around here?"

Dewey handed Adam another cookie, which he happily took. He tried a full front tooth bite now, which worked as they were getting softer, and he broke a second one in half and shoved it into his mouth, letting out a pleasurable sigh.

"Can you think fast?" Claire asked, starting to feel her throat tightening up just thinking about having to call the police or tell her dad what she'd done if they showed up before she could stop him.

Dewey didn't feel prepared to answer her. He wasn't even supposed to be working today. Suddenly, he felt like that kid in the book, like he'd swum out too far without the floor beneath him. He took a slow breath in, not because he thought it would help, but because his mom always swore that it does and he didn't have a better idea. He let it out. Dewey, he coached himself. Baboons don't laugh at each other's bottoms. Two peas in a pod. We're almost there for real now. They really did need Adam's help to solve the problem. Nothing was messed up with their plan at all. They just needed to stick with it.

"Adam," Dewey began, "We're in too deep. Claire played a practical joke that clearly has gotten out of hand. She was trying to get you back for the whole pancake-in-the-slippers-soda-can-thing and—."

"You told him 'bout that?" Adam smiled.

Claire rolled her eyes.

"So? I don't get it? You hired this guy to steal your bike and what?" Adam asked Claire.

Claire looked to Dewey to reply.

"And make a donkey out of you."

Adam tilted his head, trying to absorb what sounded an awful like it might be an insult.

Dewey tried again.

"And send you on a wild goose chase." Why did all these animals keep flying out of his mouth?

"And I'm supposed to help you now?" Adam scoffed.

"Adam! I'm going to get arrested for making a false police report!" she wailed.

"Is that a thing?" Adam asked.

Claire sobbed harder, and this time real tears came out.

"Okay, okay! Don't worry," Adam reassured. "I'll tell dad I hid your bike, and wrote that ransom note. I'll take the fall."

They had him.

"Whatever punishment you get, I'll stand by you," she promised, throwing her arms around his neck. More cookies all around, and Dewey said he'd meet them outside with the bike. He couldn't very well get the bike to go through the air ducts.

"Sure," Adam said. "But what *is* all of this, anyway?"

"This? This is my office. Dewey Fairchild, Problem Solver at your service."

He wasn't about to announce himself to Adam as a Sibling Problem Solver and blow his cover. But, as Adam and Claire made their way out of the air ducts and Dewey rolled the bike carefully down the stairs through his family's house and out the back door, it had become clear to him that was just what he'd become.

Undercover

Before the bell rang in study hall, Colin motioned for Dewey to come look at his phone. Dewey looked, and he screamed. He screamed again. There were a series of pictures of Dewey riding Claire's hot pink bike and on his head, he wore her pink, purple, and blue splatter bike helmet.

Colin laughed so hard he bent over, clutching his side.

"Give me that!" Dewey grabbed at Colin's phone. "How did you get those?"

"No! Look, don't touch!" he laughed.

"The mini-drone? You followed me?! That's amazing! And horrible! That's both amazing and horrible."

"It's awesome."

"It's fearsome!"

"I know. The possibilities are endless!"

"Okay, delete them now!"

"No! Promise. I won't post them. But they're too good. I can't delete them," Colin pleaded. "They're our first test run."

"Our first test run?"

"It was too perfect!"

"I was on a job!"

"I know, I know."

"What are you two talking about?" Seraphina plopped down and leaned in to look.

"Noth'n," Colin said. "Just some drone stuff we're working on."

At least he's loyal, Dewey thought.

"Come on, lemme see," she persisted. The bell rang.

Geez, Dewey thought. A man thinks he's minding his own business riding along on a hot pink bike in a splattered paint helmet, and the next thing you know it's gone viral.

Dewey pulled out his computer math practice problems. His mind kept drifting to everything he had to do this week. Clara had messaged she had a full case load for him they needed to start soon. What was he doing about Pooh Bear, and now Stephanie? If Pooh had told Stephanie, who would be next? He didn't have time to deal with this right now. He didn't have time not to deal with this, though. Thinking about all this was sure making it hard to focus on homework.

A small crumpled piece of paper landed in front of him and snapped him out of his ruminations.

"Can I show Seraphina the pictures?"

"Fine," Dewey wrote back. She smiled at him, making the embarrassment he was about to endure worthwhile.

"What makes pink a 'girl' color?" she asked.

"Huh?"

"I mean," she held the phone up to Colin's face so closely his eyes began to cross, "Why do you think this is a girl's bike?"

"Isn't it just obvious?" he said, adjusting the phone so he could see it. "Just look at it."

"That's just stupid, Colin."

"I don't know," Dewey said. "I just watched a bunch of YouTube videos where parents did these reveals of the new baby coming and they popped balloons with blue or pink confetti or had pink or blue frosting. Those kids knew just what they wanted. Blue for a brother and pink for a sister."

"What? No! They're already brainwashed to think that way."

Seraphina began to search on her laptop to get some proof.

"Here! Look. Before two years old, babies don't show any more interest in pink than anything else!"[1] They pick any color, not just pink."

"Before two years old, they don't know how to pick their own nose!" Colin said.

"Oh, yeah they do," Dewey laughed.

"Well, once they hit two they know what they want. And what they want is to be a boy on a blue bike."

"Ugh. Because society tells them so."

"At two years old?"

"Read."

Their teacher shot them a look which said settle down and work.

"Oh, hmm," Colin whispered, reading. "It's still funny." He held the picture up suppressing his laughter as Dewey pushed his hand down so the whole study hall class didn't see.

"Yeah, yeah, it's funny," Dewey whispered back.

"It's funny," Seraphina admitted.

"Oh, I'm so glad you could both finally agree."

---

1. https://onlinelibrary.wiley.com/doi/pdf/10.1111/j.2044-835X.2011.02027.x?sharing_unavailable=unsupported_browser&sharing_referrer=http%3A%2F%2Fwww.bbc.com%2Ffuture%2Fstory%2F20141117-the-pink-vs-blue-gender-myth

Long Tail

Dear Efren C. Disk,

I have no clue what is going on in your brain. I don't like it very much when you are mean to me. I hope that someday you will be very nice to me. I hope that someday we will be playing basketball together. It would be better for both of us if you would be a little bit nicer. I know that deep down inside you, you are defindely a griffin dor.

Love,

Louise

P.S. I hope you read this letter. A nice person would.

Dewey laughed. "A 'griffin dor'?"

"Charming, right?" Clara said as Dewey handed her back the letter.

"So, is Efren coming in today?"

"Should be here any minute."

Clara stepped into the kitchen to pull out a plate of toffee almond sandies as Dewey put his feet up on his desk and reread Louise's letter.

Suddenly Dewey heard a rumpus coming from the air ducts, like a tennis shoe in a dryer thumping around. He looked up expecting to see Efren, and for the third time this semester his brain tried to process how his expectations didn't match the reality before him.

Julie and Charles Disk came tumbling out of the ducts one on top of the other onto the lime green pillows: first Julie Disk and then her husband Charles. Mrs. Disk, whose hair had been neatly combed when she began her journey this morning to meet Dewey, now looked like she'd been through a wind storm, and her husband's pressed navy-blue suit was a now a wrinkled mess.

Mrs. Disk tried to smooth her hair. She had one leg folded behind her and the other stuck out straight ahead. She attempted to stand up and regain her composure, but found it difficult due to the pillow's ample fluff and her husband nearly landing upon her.

Dewey, himself attempting to regain composure, removed his feet from the desk, stood up, and offered Mrs. Disk a hand to pull her up.

"Mrs. Disk?" he confirmed as he heaved her off the floor pillow. Wolfie, who beyond Dewey's comprehension had somehow managed to sleep through all this ruckus, discovered their arrival and chose this moment to greet them by licking Mrs. Disk's calf.

"Yes, hello," she said, smoothing her hair again and her skirt. "Oh, what a cute dog!" The color began to return to her cheeks, which moments before looked as white as a sheet of paper.

"Wolfie, knock it off."

Mr. Disk smiled. He nodded and got onto all fours to transition his body off the big floor pillow. Wolfie took this as a game and ran over to get his miniature tennis ball, dropping it at Mr. Disk's feet.

Dewey wished Clara would hurry up and come out. She was only a few feet away, but once she got her head in the oven she got focused until she had her plate of cookies to bring out. Meanwhile, Dewey worked hard to bring all of this into clear focus.

"Please," Dewey gestured to the small loveseat they had in front of the screen. The tall wide screen served to separate the sitting area and the kitchen and provided for their movie viewing needs. "Have a seat." Were these two adults really here? How strange. Dewey felt almost out of his own body as he watched himself talk to them.

"Thank you. You got our daughter's letter," Mr. Disk began. His black rimmed rectangular glasses sat crooked on his bulb-shaped nose.

Their daughter's letter. Dewey went and grabbed it off his desk and pulled up his chair. He still felt like he was walking behind their conversation, not with it yet. He needed to catch up.

"We're at our wits' end. The only one worse to one is the other. From the moment they wake up, until the blessed moment they fall asleep, all they do is fight. I'm ready to flush them both down the toilet." Mrs. Disk threw Wolfie's ball for him. Somehow, even amid her own misery, she kept aware of that silly dog's needs. Dewey thought that was awful nice.

Mr. Disk patted her on the back.

They both looked at Dewey and waited.

The room was quiet. Light shined in through the small attic windows warming the Berber carpet and Wolfie sat down on a sunny spot.

Dewey began to feel that rudderless floating out at sea feeling. Where was Clara? Where was Efren? Why were they here?

And then Mrs. Disk spoke again.

"Can you help?"

Dewey began to feel his hands and feet again. Oh. Oh! They wanted him to solve their sibling problem? Holy cow! It wasn't Efren who was his client. It was Efren's parents!

Dewey found his sea legs and dove in.

"Sibling problems are one of my specialties. You've come to the right place. I have some paperwork for you to fill out, but if you don't mind, can you tell me how you learned of my professional services?"

Mr. and Mrs. Disk looked at one another.

"Well, I don't quite know, dear," Mr. Disk said to Mrs. Disk. "How did we end up here?"

"We grounded our son Efren for a week and he simply begged us to come meet with you since he couldn't leave the house. Was that inappropriate? Should we not have come?" Mrs. Disk asked, looking around the room for signs that he'd been expecting them.

"Oh, no, no. Not at all. Quite appropriate," Dewey said using her own words back to reassure her.

So, Efren had just told them to come in his place. He did wish Efren had asked him first.

"Just give me a sec," Dewey said, sitting down at the computer to adjust his form. Where the deuce was Clara, he thought again. He skimmed the form quickly.

'Name' and 'address,' stays, 'school' and 'grade' come out, he decided. Oh, shoot. No, he thought, hitting the 'undo typing' button. I'll just change them to 'Children's grade and school.' He put them back and fixed it. Did he need to keep the questions about how to get into the home without being noticed and top hiding places? Yes, yes, he reasoned quickly. Still needed to observe unnoticed. Okay. Change 'Parent's names and problems' to 'Siblings' and it would be all set. Geez, thought Dewey, exhaling. He hadn't realized he'd been holding his breath.

Then, he added one final line: 'Non-Disclosure Agreement: All transactions between the clients and Dewey Fairchild, Sibling Problem Solver to be kept in strict confidentiality. Please sign here:'

He let out a silent sigh, and felt himself propel forward again.

"They are going to kill one another," their father said. "And if they don't, I may."

Mrs. Disk slowly nodded in agreement.

"Here," Dewey said, handing them the form attached to a clipboard. "Just fill this out, and I'll handle the rest."

Before they left, Dewey knew where to enter, where to hide, that they had a cat, and that these parents wanted him to solve the problem of their two kids and their death-match wrestling. The Disks signed, agreeing to keep Dewey's business with their family confidential.

"I'll be there after school tomorrow," Dewey said shaking each of their hands. If Dewey ever felt grateful that he and Clara had installed the Garage Gator Electric

Motorized Lift it was now. He could only imagine the two of them crawling up on Clara's shoulders to get back into the air ducts!

"Please help yourself to the cookies you see along the way," Dewey said, aware that they'd not even been offered a single plate of cookies in Clara's absence. Where'd she go? The Gator lifted them up, and they made their way out. Dewey cringed as he heard something that sounded disturbingly like someone's head meeting solid material.

He let out a big sigh and read over some of the extra notes he'd taken in the margin of their form. "Kicking," "hitting," "name-calling," "ratting out." Dewey thought about how much easier this stakeout would be—access to a house where the parents already knew he was coming!

As if reading his mind and materializing out of nowhere, Clara spoke. "We've never had such easy access to the clients, eh boss?"

"Clara! Where have you been! Why'd you leave me hanging?"

She just stood, all of four feet and nine inches, shrugging. "You tell me, sir."

"I honestly don't know. Cookie mishap?"

"Oh, no, sir. They're in great shape. At least I think so." She offered him the plate with the toffee almond sandies. "But I'd be about as useful as a milk bucket under a bull right about then."

Dewey laughed. "Oh, you mean because bulls don't make much milk," Dewey reasoned slowly.

"Because they don't make *any*, and because those two had enough to work through without trying to figure out how I fit into the mix."

"Ha! Mix! Get it! Mix! Cookies."

Clara smiled but feigned insult, furrowing her brows. "Always from scratch, sir."

"Right, of course. I meant it like to stir, not in the Betty Crocker way."

"Ah. That *is* a mix up."

Dewey chuckled and smiled.

"Seriously, Clara, I was as nervous as, as . . ." Dewey paused to try and come up with a good Clara-like expression.

"As nervous as a long-tailed cat in a room full of rocking chairs?" she asked.

"Yes!" he nodded wholeheartedly. "Yes! That's right." She laughed warmly and put her hands on his shoulders. These days she had to reach up to do just that.

"You did it, though! Your tail is fully intact. Shall we see what comes next?"

Yellow Tail

The only thing better than some kid bringing you snacks on a stakeout is some kid's parent bringing them to you. Dewey sat on a long bench with a blue cushion in the mudroom, which provided him ample space to hide out next to the kitchen and to stretch way out. The long narrow bench ran the length of the wall with large square pillows along the way for Dewey to rest his back against. Underneath the bench were cubbies with wicker baskets for shoes, scarves, hats, and a bunch of other stuff. Some cubbies had no baskets and just shoes lined up. Above Dewey's head jackets and coats hung on two big hooks. On the other wall across from him sat two large front-loading silver machines, the washer with the door slightly open, Mrs. Disk explained, to avoid mildew. There was a large country sink and a broom closet. A long blue and white rug ran the length of the room. A door led out to the back yard while another one led to the kitchen.

"I think this will be a perfect spot for you, Dewey, if you don't mind sharing the space with Pumpkin." Pumpkin was the Disks' orange and white tabby. His cat box also resided in what otherwise, Dewey rapidly began to think, would make a perfect home away from home for himself.

"There's a comforter in this basket, some guest slippers if your feet get cold. Here's a little snack for you. I hope you like sushi?"

Sushi?! Yes, indeed. Dewey thought this case might take a while to sort out. He might even need to observe extra hours.

"Thanks, Mrs. Disk!"

"Sure, Dewey. We're just so grateful. And really, please. Call me Julie."

"Thank you, Julie." Dewey eyed Pumpkin who jumped up on the bench having gotten a whiff of his yellowtail.

Mrs. Disk nudged Pumpkin down. "Okay, then. The kids should be home any minute now for lunch. They never come in the back unless it's raining, so we'll be fine. And no one is volunteering to change the cat box, you can be sure. You should be well situated here. Oh, and here's the WC if you need it," she smiled opening a door to a little half bath right off the laundry room.

Wow, thought Dewey. I really could move in.

Dewey propped up a couple pillows behind his back and ate his sushi. He tore open the little packet of soy sauce and used the lid as a bowl to mix in some wasabi. He sat up on the bench and took a selfie with a piece of California roll hanging out of his mouth. "#onthejob," he messaged Colin.

He opened the can of bubbly water she'd given him and washed it all down just as he heard the family coming in the front door. He could smell what he concluded to be hotdogs sizzling in butter from the kitchen. What Dewey witnessed next seemed to him a rather uneventful lunch. Mrs. Disk needed to drop the kids and run out for something, and Mr. Disk fed the kids hot dogs, carrot sticks, salad, and milk. He asked about the game. They answered. It all seemed rather humdrum to Dewey. He sat on the bench petting the cat wondering what the fuss was all about.

"Clear your places before you leave the room, please," Mr. Disk reminded. Then all was quiet. Dewey and Pumpkin had no choice but to settle into a little cat nap.

Dewey was just settling into this part of the job with Pumpkin on his chest when he suddenly heard the yells.

"Get out! Get ouuttt!! Louise! Mom!"

"Ow! Efren! Stop it!"

Pumpkin sprung off his chest, and Dewey covered his face for protection.

He stuck his head out of the door, looked both ways, and headed around the corner to get a better look.

Louise had one shoe stuck in Efren's door and Efren was on the other side doing his almighty best to close it. The fact that her foot had gotten in the way was only making him more upset. His goal was to shut her out. Her goal, originally to get into his room to be with her older brother, now came down to the more fundamental drive to get her foot back.

Mr. Disk pounded on the door. "Efren. Open this door! Louise's foot is trapped!"

"Serves her right!" he yelled from the other side of the door.

"Mom!" wailed Louise, more from the injustice than actual pain as thankfully the tennis shoe's rubber helped cushion the ever-tightening compression between her foot and the door.

"Mom's not home. Efren!" Mr. Disk hollered again, pushing his weight against the door. Efren had pushed a chair under the door knob, so the door popped open but then closed again on Louise's shoe and that caused some discomfort. Louise began to scream now.

"Aaaahhh!"

"Oh, for Pete's sake!" Mr. Disk said, untying Louise's shoe and pulling her foot out as the door slammed shut. Mr. Disk took his daughter to the couch, inspected her foot, and assured her it was more pain of rejection than injury that was afoot.

Now that she'd stopped screaming for a minute, Dewey took in Louise's shoulder-length wavy brown hair, worn in a ponytail that didn't hide her hate for brushing out knots. When she wasn't bursting out in tears, she had a smile that made her cheeks get round like pink taffies. Right now, Dewey thought her cheeks looked more like warm pink puddles. She had on a t-shirt today that said, 'This is one for the books!'

"Why did you go in there? You know he doesn't like that."

"I just wanted to ask him something."

"What?"

"I don't know."

"Louise." Mr. Disk's reproach caused Louise to burst out in tears.

"Why does he hate me so much?! I hate him!" She ran into her room.

Mr. Disk then knocked and entered his son's room. "Efren Charles," he began.

"Dad!" he objected. "I don't want her in my room!" At seven-eighths of an inch, Efren's hair was a number seven cut. If he'd had his way it would have been a number four. He loved all things military and police, and wanted his dirty blond hair to be in a buzz. His mother had other ideas for him, saying things like, "But you have such nice hair," and that she didn't really care for how it made his ears "glow" when he stood in the light.

"I am aware," Mr. Disk sighed. "But you sure have a funny way of showing it by trapping her in your doorway. You're almost twice her height, Efren."

"But she—"

"I don't want to hear it. Your mother and I will decide how to handle this when she gets home. For now, she will stay out of your room and you will leave your door open."

"What?! NO!"

"Don't test me, this is my door. I'll take it off the hinges and you won't even have one. Your mother will be home and you are going to the dentist in an hour." He stormed out, embarrassed all of this had just happened before Dewey's observing eyes. Still, he felt hopeful Dewey might be able to help. Somehow.

Shotgun

It had been a while since Dewey had taken an undercover car ride. He got plenty of notice though, and they set him up in the back row of their Explorer under a tarp. They were set to leave at 2:20 for a 3:00 appointment, so Dewey settled himself by 2:15.

"Shotgun. I call shotgun!" Louise dashed toward the car like she was in a relay race.

"No, I call it!" Efren's long legs hightailed it after her.

"No, I said it first."

"I called it!"

"You didn't call it."

"It doesn't matter if you called it. I need more room, Louise!"

"That's not fair. MO-OM! I called it."

Dewey thought their scuffle might have dented the car. Sure sounded like it.

"Efren, she called it. I heard her. Get in the back, please. You can ride up front on the way home."

"She's not even old enough to ride up front!" he objected.

"Am, too! I weigh enough now!"

"This is bull—"

"Efren . . ." his mother turned around and faced him raising a pointer finger in warning.

"—-Loney. Bul-loney," he grumbled and kicked the back of Louise's seat hard.

"MOM!"

"Shall we just try to arrive to Dr. McCandlish's office in one piece?" their mother asked, pulling out of the driveway.

Dewey observed through the crack in the seat as Louise slowly and incrementally moved her seat back inch by inch, crowding Efren more and more. With each scoot back, he rewarded her with his knee pushing and jamming into the back of her seat. This went on in silence as Mrs. Disk drove for maybe all of forty-five seconds. Finally, when Louise had moved her seat back as much as humanly possible, Efren madly reached over her seat with both hands. Whether it was to grab her neck in a choke hold, or haul her whole body over the seat into the back Dewey couldn't tell, but the car came to an abrupt halt that lurched him forward and locked his seatbelt.

"Out. Everybody out!"

"Out?"

They were pulled over in a parking lot nowhere near the dentist's office.

Louise didn't move. Efren began to loosen his seatbelt.

"What do you think you're doing?"

"But you said—"

"Don't be ridiculous. No one is going anywhere. I'm not moving this car until this incessant fighting stops. You two want your teeth to rot and fall out of your heads? That's just fine with me. We can just sit here and never go to the dentist, ever. We can live here for all I care."

Like her son's bedroom door, she was threatening to come unhinged.

Louise moved her seat up.

"That's better."

The rest of the car ride remained silent until Mrs. Disk let out a long sigh and turned on some music.

"Can I pick the station?" Louise asked, turning past numbers.

"Oh! There, there! Stop there!" Efren said.

Louise kept moving higher up the numbers past the song Efren liked.

"Louise! Go back!" he yelled, leaning up trying to reach the dial with his long arms.

"I'm picking!" she objected. "Mom!"

He flicked her on the back of the head.

"Ow!"

Just then, Dewey's phone vibrated. 'SOS' from Clara. This couldn't be good.

SOS

"No. No, no, no, no, no. You guys can't be here!" Dewey paced back and forth in his office. "I already told you that."

Dewey had really hoped Stephanie and Pooh's discovery of his office would somehow just go away. But here they were again in his office. Pooh seemed to have already polished off a plate of cookies and milk, and sat on the floor coloring a picture.

"Hi, Dewey! I'm drawing Wolfie!"

Dewey gasped and sighed with distress, then looked at Clara who just shrugged.

"Stephanie, what do you want?"

"Tell me what you're doing up here? What's all this?"

This situation wasn't going away. He was right in the middle of a case, and the situation just wasn't going away.

He sat down at his desk and sighed again. "What do you want to know?"

"Why are you two up here?"

Dewey felt prickly.

"Working," replied Dewey coolly.

"On what?"

"Do you like his tail? I made it like a fan!"

"It's nice, Pooh," Dewey said.

"Very nice," Clara smiled. "I never thought about it, but it's true. His tail does look like a white feathery fan."

"I'm making it orange."

"So??" Stephanie asked looking around.

"So, what?" Dewey growled.

Clara came up behind Dewey. She rested her hands on his shoulder.

Argh! Why is this happening?! Dewey looked at his phone to see the time. By now the Disks would have left the dentist. He texted Mrs. Disk. He had ducked out of there as soon as he'd had a chance.

```
got lots of data

will be back in touch soon
```

He couldn't even think straight right now. He had no

idea how he was going to solve the Disk sibling issue. He didn't have the space to think about it right now.

"Dewey?"

"What?"

"What do you guys do up here?"

He tried to quiet the buzzing in his head.

"We solve problems."

"Like what kinds of problems?"

"All kinds, I guess."

"Can I help?" Pooh asked.

"So, you're just up here solving problems? Really?"

"Really."

"Like what, for example?"

"I don't know. I'm working on some kids who all they do is fight. A while ago, I helped these kids when their teacher was boring them to death." Annoyed. Dewey felt annoyed.

"That's kind of cool."

Dewey felt a little less annoyed. Approval from Stephanie? He almost wanted to tell her more.

"Can you guys go now?"

"Sure."

"I don't wanna go," Pooh said.

"Come on, Pooh. We gotta go."

Dewey felt a warm grateful relief swell behind his eyes and he softened.

"Thank you," he said.

"No problem."

"We're coming back, though, right?" he could hear Pooh Bear asking as she made her way through the ducts. "Right? Right?"

"OMG! How am I supposed to get anything done this way?!"

"I do hope it was okay to call you, sir. I wasn't quite sure how you wanted to handle the sister situation."

"Well, if you don't know, I sure don't," Dewey threw his hands up in the air and let them drop hard. "I've got my hands full with Efren and Louise and their parents are counting on me coming up with something. Efren thought I'd be there for just him. Now I'm supposed to help them both. I gotta spend some time going through all of my notes about them and figure something out."

"I'm sure you'll come up with something, sir."

"Hmm. You always say that," Dewey said.

"And you always do."

"Do I?"

"Like a roll with butter."

Wolfie Needs a Diaper Change

Dewey spent the afternoon going back to reading online about sibling problems and possible solutions. There were hundreds, maybe even thousands of blogs on the topic.

"Here's one. She does a 'job jar' where she puts in chores and if her kids fight they have to pick out a chore and do it. This one is like the jar idea, but makes them pay money anytime her kids say something mean.

"'Separate siblings until they miss one another.' 'Force them to be together until they love one another,'" Dewey continued reading. "That's kind of like those sewn together twin shirts. Haha! This dad makes his two sons stand nose to nose, or toe to toe until they get nice. That just seems cruel, doesn't it?"

"Try it yourself sometime with Stephanie or Pooh and let me know how it goes."

"No thanks!"

Whole sections were devoted to who gets to sit in the front seat of the car! Turns out the middle seat in the back also posed family problems. Pooh's car seat was there so he'd never actually thought about that, but *he* wouldn't want to sit on that hump. Parents in the online forums said they had kids take turns every other day, every other week. But then the kids argued about whose day of the week it was.

"That's funny," Dewey chuckled. "Nope. There's no way out of this. Kids are just going to fight and tear one another apart."

"If I may, sir. Why don't we start with your own sibling problem?"

"I have a sibling problem?"

She smiled.

"Oh, you mean Pooh and Stephanie coming here? I don't have time to deal with that. I have to focus on my real problems to solve."

Clara smiled again.

She handed him a cookie.

"Oh, *alright*," he moped.

"Here's your chance," she said.

"Huh?"

Before she further explained, down plopped none other than one Pooh Bear.

"Argh! Are you kidding?!"

"Don't be mad, Dewey! You said! You said I could come back."

"When? When did I say that?" he asked the air.

"So, what?" Dewey asked Clara. "I give her a chore from a jar? Hug her toe-to-toe for three hours? What?!" He was getting exasperated.

"Why," Clara whispered into his ear, "don't you just spend a little time with her?"

He looked aghast. And confused. He had a million things to do. Clara nodded. And walked out.

Why did she always do that?

"O-kaay, do you want to do something together?"

"Here?!" Pooh clapped her hands together. "Yay!"

"O-kaay, what do you want to do?"

"Let's play with Wolfie. I can be Wolfie's mom, and you can be his dad, and he can be our baby!"

"Wake up dog, we're playing."

Wolfie, who ordinarily would already be running around when someone arrived, conveniently lay curled up like a black and white comma in his bed.

"I guess you'd better go rouse him. Here, I'll make the baby his bottle and you can bring it to him." Dewey pretended to make Wolfie a bottle and handed it to his sister.

Pooh, looking quite earnest, took the "bottle" from him and walked over to Wolfie.

"Here, baby," she said in a high soft voice. "It's time for your bottle."

Wolfie lifted his head expecting something, *anything*, really, other than nothing, and he put his head back down.

"Oh. He's so cute." She tried to pick him up but he wasn't helping, so Dewey went over and heaved him up.

"Oh! That's my big boy," Dewey grunted. "Come to Papa." He picked Wolfie up like a baby and put him over his shoulder.

"We have ta' change the baby's diaper," Pooh said.

"Oh boy," Dewey laughed.

Wolfie, looking confused as she attempted to lay him on his back, began to wriggle. No belly rub, no dice. He rolled back and stood on his four legs.

"Aww! No fair!"

"Why don't we try doing what he wants for a bit. Might work better?" Dewey suggested. "You want to give him some water and then we can play keep-away with his Skunky?"

Pooh carefully filled up his water bowl and they played for a while with Pooh laughing and running back and forth almost as much as Wolfie. Wolfie began to pant and walk, and Pooh gave a yawn. The whole thing lasted about fifteen minutes, tops.

Then she headed for the Gator.

"Wolfie can't play on there."

"I know," she said. Though he had no idea how she could possibly know such a thing. "Bye, Dewey!" She stopped and turned back to kiss Wolfie on the head. Dewey just stood there staring at her. Then she hopped on the Gator.

"Dewey," she said. "Put it up."

"Oh, right. See ya."

Up and out she went.

Dewey settled on the couch. "She left! So fast!"

"Indeed," Clara said.

Road Plan

All the kids called it the Big Ship park due to the gigantic play ship in the middle of the play area. Dewey and his friends used to climb on that ship, pretending they were pirates, or that great white sharks swam beneath them in the sand. These days, they rarely hung out where the swings and play structures stood. Instead it was the large grassy field and open spaces that occupied their recreation.

"What do we do?" Seraphina asked.

They had gone there after school. Dewey and Colin wanted to do some more mini-drone photo work and Seraphina and Elinor joined in.

"It's going to be hard to top last week's pics," Colin said, ribbing Dewey about the pink bicycle.

"Ha-ha," Dewey said sarcastically. "Let's take some of you this time."

"Okay." They walked up the stairs to scout a good spot.

"Hey! Seraphina! Elinor! You're lagging!" They had not followed them up the stairs.

"Never mind," Colin said. "They'll catch up."

Colin and Dewey headed over to the little kids' play area, and began to film Colin on the swings.

"Try to fly it as high as I get. Then see if you can lower it as I jump off."

They tried that take a few times.

"Not bad!" Dewey played it back. "Battery's low now. Where *are* they?"

They walked over to the other side of the park along a winding path.

"This is where I met Wolfie for the first time," Colin said. "Remember?"

"Oh, yeah," Dewey laughed. "Clara walked right through here where the signs say no dogs allowed. Wolfie. So cute and little then."

"What the—" Colin couldn't believe what he was seeing. Seraphina and Elinor were at the bottom of four stairs with a, could it be?

"They've got the Parrot Jumping Sumo! No way!"

Dewey and Colin ran over.

The Parrot Jumping Sumo was a mini-drone that jumped almost three feet high and went up to almost four-and-a-half miles an hour. It had two big wheels like a monster truck, and a center that looked like a space capsule.

"Whose is this? Where'd you get it? How's it work? Can I try?"

They laughed.

"Mine. eBay. We'll show you. Sure," Elinor said, laughing some more at Colin.

"Why didn't you tell us?!"

"You didn't ask," Seraphina smiled, putting her hand on Dewey's shoulder.

"Here. I'll show you. Just push here to go forward," Elinor said, holding her phone, "and tilt it like this to go left or right."

"What's this button?"

"Turn 180. But 'spin' is the coolest."

Colin hit 'spin' and it whipped around in a circle like a top, making a computer sound like BB-8.

'Tap' produced a quick jerk.

"Eh," Dewey wrinkled his nose.

'Slow Shake' moved left, right, left, but made a sound like a baby kitten mewing for milk.

"Cute, right?" Seraphina nodded, agreeing with herself.

"Lemme try," Dewey stuck his hand out to Colin for Elinor's phone.

"Try 'Metronome' or 'Spin Jump.'" Dewey hit 'Spin Jump' and the Parrot spun fast and leapt off the ground.

"Whoa! Give it back!" Colin extended his hand.

"The battery's low. Let us show you 'Road Plan' and what we just made!"

Elinor gestured for Dewey and Colin to sit on the bench.

"It's a color walk. We picked a color. Blue. Because girls can like blue, *as you know*," Seraphina paused, emphasizing her words. "We walked all around here looking for blue stuff."

"We mapped the best stuff using 'Road Plan,'" Elinor added.

"What's that?" Colin asked, extending his hand to see her phone again. She gently pushed his hand down and smiled before answering him.

"You map out directions it goes. Like tell it to go straight four feet, turn right, take a picture, jump, then take a picture."

"Coooool."

"This changes everything!" Colin said, putting his hand out again.

"Soon," Elinor said. "Soon."

He dropped his hand.

Colin and Dewey watched as the Parrot moved past a blue bench, hopped up, and took a still shot of a blue recycle bin.

"I have another battery. You guys can give it a try."

"Yesss!" Colin said picking up the Parrot.

"Go on a color walk. Pink."

"Nooo!" Colin said, setting it back down like it had germs.

"I just did that ride," Dewey said.

"Don't be juvenile. See if you can beat our blue."

"Oh, fine. You're on," Colin said.

"Good!" Elinor smiled. "You can start with that piece of pink gum stuck under your shoe."

Dewey looked down, picked his right foot up and saw nothing. He lifted his left and saw a long stringy pink wad stretch from his rubber sole to the pavement.

"Did you plant that?!" Dewey asked, amazed.

"Don't move," Colin said. "We need to film you as the first stop."

"How am I going to help look for pink stuff if I don't move?"

Free Ride

"Take off your shoe and leave it there so we can use it when we're ready!"

Dewey sighed, taking off his left shoe. "The things I do for you, people."

Dewey and Colin ran around looking for the color pink.

"There's nothing, and this is dumb! Let's just hook this baby up and let it roll!"

"Thank you!" Dewey agreed. "Let's put it in 'free ride' mode and do an obstacle course," Dewey said, looking around for things the Parrot could maneuver and grabbing his left shoe.

They gathered empty soda cans and stacked them up in a pyramid, dragged a log over, and found a baseball hat.

Soon, Seraphina and Elinor joined in gathering leaves and making a path for the Parrot to follow.

"Lead it to the stairs, jump down, and then follow the path!"

"Here! Ha!" Dewey said. "Pink!" Someone had discarded a piece of pink cellophane in a cardboard box from a gift or maybe a cupcake.

Dewey shoved the cellophane in his pocket. Maybe they'd use it at the end somehow, like the finish line or something.

They worked together and at the end had a short video that lasted all of thirty-seconds and took them almost two hours to create. The little Parrot droid jumped out of the cardboard box, hit the ground, spun around like an insane top, did a two-foot vertical jump, and headed off down the path of leaves.

"Wait!" Colin yelled, running alongside it two steps ahead as Dewey worked the controller. He scattered some purple jacaranda flowers he'd grabbed along the ground like he was a fairy sprinkling pixie dust. "Ha ha! Purple! Okay?! Pink's closest kinswoman!"

"You're a goofball, Colin!" Seraphina laughed.

"No, I'm Greaseball."

The mini-droid busted down the soda can pyramid.

"Whoa!" they all yelled.

It continued to roll under the bench, and a nearby squirrel scurried up a tree.

"Aw, poor little guy," Dewey said.

"We should do a whole thing with it filming squirrels! It's totally eye level to them," Elinor said as she chased behind it, jumping down the three long stairs.

The Parrot wound its way along more of their path, and pulled up to take its final bow like a little one-eyed droid in a black tux on the shiny pink cellophane red carpet.

"That's called an undulation. Cool move, huh?"

Just then, a small kid being pulled by a beautiful golden retriever made his way through their obstacle course. To think that Wolfie and he were even the same kind of animal, members of the genus *Canis*, seemed hard to believe. Wolfie was a sturdy fellow. His features were symmetrical, too. They both had pink tongues, with mouths that smiled, and warm brown expressive eyes, and black teddy bear noses. This dog though, running through their obstacle course trailing a small child behind him, spoke sleek and symmetrical engineered beauty, like a new rose-gold iPhone. Wolfie spoke more manufactured fluff-ball cuteness—like, say, Amazon's Echo Dot.

"Stop, Oli!" he shouted as the dog dragged him along on a heavy rope.

Too late. Their Parrot was a sitting duck.

Before any of them knew what had happened Oliver's mouth came chopping down around the mini-Parrot like it was a tennis ball.

Solver Heal Thyself

"Let go, boy! Let go!" Oliver's boy tried grabbing the Parrot, but the two wheels just hung out the side of the dog's mouth.

"I'm sorry!" he tried to pry it out.

The dog wasn't chewing on it, but he wouldn't let go of it, either.

"Don't pull too hard," Dewey warned. "It might snap."

"Oh, man. My parents are going to kill me," Elinor said. "I just got it."

"Hang on a second," Colin said, digging into his pant pockets. "Who has a dollar? Quick. Oh, wait. I do. Don't let that dog run!"

Colin ran, though, and within about a minute and a half came back with a Screwball Cherry ice cream. He peeled off the paper top and held the cone under the dog's mouth to lick.

"Here, dog."

The dog dropped the Parrot and he took a big bite of it.

"Here," he said, holding the Parrot gingerly between his thumb and forefinger to avoid the dog slobber.

"Thank you!" Elinor sang.

"Better take your dog away from us," Dewey said to the kid, leading the dog away with the ice cream.

"Yeah. So sorry!" the kid said as he took over holding the ice cream to lead the dog away.

When the dog got out of the park, they tested to make sure the Parrot still worked. It jumped and spun without incident.

Elinor threw her arms around Colin.

"Thank you!" she said again.

"Fast thinking!" Seraphina said.

"Ha! The color!" Colin pointed to the melting dark pink puddle on the ground.

"Nice!" Dewey nodded. "Screwball for the win!"

Later that evening, Dewey wandered into Stephanie's room. He hardly ever went in there these days.

"What's up, Dewsters?" she asked, looking up from her homework.

"Do you remember when Mom and Dad told you they were having another baby and they were adopting me?"

"Uh huh."

"What do you remember?"

"Well, they bought me a doll so I wouldn't pull your head off."

"Were you jealous?"

"I don't remember. I hated sharing my stuff with you. Freaking broke everything."

"Really?"

"Really."

He just sat there on her bed, watching her.

"Like right now. You're nice and all, but I'm kind of busy and you're still here. I don't wanna hurt your feelings or anything, so I'm still talking to ya. But I'm kinda busy. And you're still kinda here."

"Right," he nodded slowly.

"Right what?" she asked.

"Nothing," he said. It never occurred to him that he might bother her the way Pooh bothered him.

"Dewey. Done here?"

"Oh, yeah. Thanks. Sorry. Close your door?"

"Please."

He'd been hoping to ask her if she had any ideas about how to help the Disks. Why not? She'd walked into his office. Might as well use her superior brain. He also was hoping to ask her if she'd ever gotten detention. She wasn't having any of it, though.

Too bad Pooh didn't have any good ideas. She'd be more than happy to help. Just then a text came in from Mrs. Disk.

> Louise just sailed Efren's Lego in the bathtub and Efren stuffed her doll head-first in the toilet. Coming back soon?!
>
> Yes

He'd go back, but he wished he felt a little bit closer to his game plan.

A Great Quantity of Wind

It turned out that Pooh did give Dewey an idea. It came to him as he ate a plateful of nachos in the mudroom, listening to Louise make her case for taking Efren's Legos for a morning ride on the high seas.

"It wasn't my fault. My fingers were greasy 'cause of the pepperoni," she explained.

"You had pizza?" Mr. Disk clarified.

"Right."

"She has to take all of the pepperoni off her pizza and put it in a pile and then walk around eating it. Her fingers get all greasy and disgusting. She goes in my room and grabs my Lego!" Efren yelled.

"You'll get your turn," Mrs. Disk said, trying to keep

the tempers calm. "So you have pepperoni fingers and go get the Lego?"

"Right! I got the Lego, so that's why they got all greasy but that was a mistake because I didn't want them greasy, just to play with, and I had to wash them, so I put them in the bath, and then Efren put Molly in the toilet!!" Hot tears began to run down her face.

"You're not supposed to be in my room! Mom! Dad! Why's she touching my Lego!? My LEGO! She doesn't even LIKE LEGO!! And she put it in the bathtub?! I'll never get it rebuilt right. Do something to her! Now she's going to cry like the baby she is and just get away with it."

Dewey was confused. Mrs. Disk's text had said Louise took Efren's pirate Lego for a sail in the bathtub. She had the details wrong. Louise didn't want to play with Efren's stuff. She wanted to play with him. That kid needed to play with his sister for fifteen minutes before she destroyed all his stuff. Fifteen minutes of playing with Wolfie and Pooh had sent her on her way for him, maybe it would help them, too.

Dewey found it funny, perfect almost, that his own fingers were covered in grease from the nachos as this idea came to him. He sucked it off his pointer finger and gave Pumpkin a little string of cheese that clung to the plate.

"You RUINED MOLLY!" she screamed. "Lego's waterproof! Molly's all ruined forever! Molly!" she wailed.

Now, how was he going to get Efren to see the benefit? How had Clara done it?

As he sat propped up on the bench, knees up, back against the corner of the wall, he tried to think about that saying, something about prevention and it how was worth it in the long run. That was the basic idea. He tried searching for it but didn't have enough of the right words. He braved trying Stephanie again.

> Dewey: `whats that famous quote about prevention`
>
> Stephanie: `huh??`
>
> D: `famous guy`
>
> S: `franklin?`
>
> D: `maybe`
>
> S: `ounce of prevention...`

Yes! That was it. She always knew. He searched Benjamin Franklin and an ounce of prevention and found what he had almost been remembering from who knows where. "An ounce of prevention is worth a pound of cure." That was the idea he needed to sell. Dewey picked at the cheese at the bottom of the plate, reading more about Benjamin Franklin and his saying.

Franklin had visited Boston and seen that they were better prepared to fight fires than they were where he lived in Philadelphia. So he pretended he was an old man and wrote an anonymous letter to his local newspaper, saying how their firefighting practices in Philadelphia stink, and if they'd be so kind, they should take the following "hints" on how to make it better. 'Cause he could hardly be expected to help his neighbors if they have a fire. He was old! And his hands were all brittle and arthritic!

It was written in that way people used to talk forever ago, plus he was pretending to be some old guy, so that probably wasn't helping things, but Dewey got the idea:

An ounce of prevention . . . avoid the fire in the first place. Then you don't find yourself faced with waiting for a team of younger guys to rescue you from a burning building. One way he said would be for folks not to walk around from room to room with open shovels full of embers dropping like the crumbs of some kid eating a cookie without a plate. Otherwise, the next thing you know, you're trapped in a burning house leaping out of your window . . . and, too bad you didn't put a lid on that shovel.

Put a lid on your shovel. Put a lid on your sister! That's not a bad motto, he chuckled to himself. Fire prevention.

That's a pretty good working idea. He liked it. This inspired him to see what other wisdom Benjamin Franklin had.

Ha! He said, "Haste makes waste?" I had no idea that was Ben Franklin, Dewey thought. He read on. "Honesty is the best policy" was his, too? "Early to bed, early to rise, makes a man healthy, wealthy, and wise." Dewey knew that one was his from school. He read on, reading a bunch of other great sayings, and following the links to different pages until he stumbled upon this nugget—an essay he wrote in 1780 to the Royal Academy of Brussels: "It is universally well known, That in digesting our common Food, there is created or produced in the Bowels of human Créatures, a great Quantity of Wind." Dewey laughed! Benjamin Franklin wrote an essay on farting! Why didn't they teach *this* stuff in school?!

"Dewey?" Mrs. Disk poked her head in the mudroom.

He'd gotten caught up in Benjamin Franklin's proposal that they invent some drug to mix into food so when people fart it doesn't stink as much. Thomas Edison invented the light bulb. Eli Whitney invented the cotton gin. Benjamin Franklin his bifocals. But turning farts into perfume? No one had mentioned that! All caught up in these thoughts, he jumped when Mrs. Disk entered. Lost in his thoughts, he'd forgotten where he was and the mission at hand.

"Sorry," she said. "I didn't mean to startle you."

"Oh, no, that's okay."

"Well, it's just a mess," she sighed and sat down, picking up the completely clean plate.

"Those were really good, thanks so much."

She didn't seem to hear him. "Charles put each kid in their room to cool off."

"I've got some ideas," Dewey said. "I'd like to pull it all together and meet with you both. Tomorrow afternoon in my office?" As he suggested it, Dewey pictured them squeezing their way again through the air ducts and thought better of it.

"Actually, if you'd like, I can come here."

She nodded slowly as if her mind were elsewhere.

"Mrs. Disk? Do you want me to come here?"

"Yes," she said still a bit distractedly. "Yes." She said again this time looking at him with more focus. "Let's do it now, shall we?"

Now? Now! What? No, he wasn't ready.

"Perfect. I'll get Charles. Let's meet in the yard. It's lovely out. The kids are in their rooms, and we'll have some privacy."

"Um,"

She looked at him waiting.

"Okay," he said slowly.

"Just go out the back door, and we'll be out in a few minutes."

Dewey sat alone on the bench. He swallowed hard.

There was no time to consult with Clara. No time to finish percolating. He thought of Jedd, all alone out in that lake treading water, with no bottom below.

"Okay," he said again, this time as he slapped his legs and stood up.

The yard was bigger than he expected. A long stretch of green grass ran along the length of the house with a soccer net at the end. A patio lined the side closest to the house with an outdoor couch, a long dining set, and an outdoor BBQ. Dewey sat down at the table, hoping for a few minutes more to gather his thoughts. Mr. Disk came out with a tray of glasses and Mrs. Disk with a pitcher of what looked like lemonade.

"Here we are," she said pleasantly. "We'll take nothing short of you rescuing us." She set out the tall iced-filled glasses as her husband poured the lemonade.

"That, or build me a guesthouse. I can't take it anymore," Mr. Disk said.

Then silence as they both looked at him with hope and anticipation.

Dewey took a swig of lemonade and wiped off his upper lip.

"Well," he began treading water, "Perhaps Benjamin Franklin said it best." He pulled out his phone and went to his history, searching for something, anything that might help him.

"'Fish and visitors stink in three days.'"

"Well, I suppose that's true," Mr. Disk said, laughing.

"Right," Dewey said. "So, maybe that's true for siblings because we, er, um, they just end up being together a lot, you know?"

"Yes, yes," Mrs. Disk leaned in, interested in Dewey's observations.

Hang on, man, Dewey thought, sensing there might be a shore out there somewhere.

"And," he glanced down at his phone again, scanning it quickly. "Of course there's also, 'He that sows Thorns, should never go barefoot.'"

Dewey had no good idea where to go with this one. He felt his face flush hot red.

"Right . . . right!" Mr. Disk nodded slowly. "The kids treat one another badly but they actually get hurt themselves in the process. Is that it?"

"Right," Dewey said nodding up and down. He felt one of his feet hit the bottom of his imaginary lake, and knew he could bring himself back to shore. "I think so. Efren wants to be left alone, but Louise wants his attention. "

"Yes, that's right," Mrs. Disk nodded, pouring more lemonade into Dewey's glass. At this rate, Dewey thought, he was going to make a lake of his own soon.

Dewey continued. "Efren pricks Louise just by not wanting to be with her. Then she gets all in his business, messes something up, that pricks him and he pricks her back."

Both Disks nodded their heads so hard Dewey thought one of them might lose one.

He looked down at his phone again.

"But," he said, raising his pointer finger sagely, "He that sows thorns' really shouldn't walk around barefoot. So, I think," Dewey concluded bringing it all home, "if we could just get Efren to give her some focused time she'd back off."

"And that fish wouldn't stink so much!"

"Right," Dewey said.

Working with parents is cool, Dewey thought. Just give them some string and they help you sew the whole outfit!

Mrs. Disk jumped up and threw her arms around him. Mr. Disk shook his hand again and again so many times Dewey felt it moving long after he'd returned to the office.

"That's terrific, boss," Clara smiled warmly when he recounted the details. She handed him a glass of cool milk and a plate of German chocolate-cake cookies.

"Right?" Dewey said, popping one in his mouth. "I was just hoping I could pull it all off!"

"'He that lives upon hope, dies farting.'"

"What?!" Dewey burst out laughing. He had to catch the milk from spraying out of his mouth. "I can't believe you just said that, Clara!"

"I didn't. Benjamin Franklin did."

Pig Iron

Dewey and his friends sat out on the benches at school. The grass was still damp. It was late May, and June Gloom had arrived. June Gloom—that distinctly Southern California weather pattern where the air has begun to get warmer, but the Pacific Ocean is still cold, resulting in condensation like a soda can out of the fridge on a hot day. Clouds, kind of drippy, wet, and gray, hung low as a marine layer all morning and would burn off in the afternoon. June Gloom weather forecasts always sounded the same—"Morning low clouds giving way to sunny skies, highs will be in the mid-seventies (or low eighties)." Dewey had heard it his whole life.

"What *is* this? I thought California was warm and

sunny! I could have stayed in Washington if I wanted gray drizzle days like this," Elinor said.

"June Gloom," Dewey said.

"May Gray," Seraphina nodded.

"No sky July. August Fogust!" laughed Colin.

"What? This goes on all summer?!"

"Stop. You're scaring her."

"Usually just the beginning of summer," Seraphina laughed. "It burns off by lunch. You gotta bring a sweatshirt in the morning."

"In California? Ugh."

"I know. It frizzes my hair," Seraphina said, twisting her long wavy brown hair into a knot.

"Me, too," laughed Colin.

"I like it. Not too hot that way. September's summer. Ridiculously hot as soon as school gets going. And no air conditioning."

"What?" asked Elinor.

"California. Don't need it, I guess. We do, though. We sweat like pigs in there."

"They're getting air soon," Seraphina said. "It's in the new plans."

"Do pigs sweat?" Dewey asked.

"Huh?"

"You know, do pigs sweat?"

"I don't think so. Isn't that why they roll around in the mud? To cool off?"

"That's right."

"This is such a Dewey conversation."

"Well, then it makes no sense. Why would you 'sweat like a pig' when they don't sweat?"

"Takis. Gimme one!"

"Take."

"Ah ha! Nothing to do with pigs," Seraphina said, reading from her phone. "Pig iron. It sweats when it gets hot."

"Disappointing. I wanted it to be about pigs."

Elinor held up a picture she'd been drawing. It was a little manga girl with big round eyes wearing a pink pig hoodie costume. The top of the page said, "June Gloomy."

"How'd you do that so fast?!"

Elinor shrugged. "It's ironic. June in California is gloomy, but I'm feeling pretty happy to be here."

Why Not

Two weeks later, satisfied customers, Efren and Louise's parents offered to pay Dewey for his services. As long as he'd been in the business of problem solving, the idea of earning money for it had never once presented itself.

"I don't know how we can ever truly repay you," Mr. Disk wrote in an email. "How much do we owe you for a job well done?"

"Owe me?" Dewey asked Clara. "That's a funny thought. Grown-ups pay for these services!"

"Yes, I suppose they do."

"I don't know, Clara. They also need a whole new entry system," he said, looking up at the ducts and

Garage Gator. Grown-ups crawling along air ducts was not ideal.

"That's true, too, sir."

"Can't we just keep things as they are?"

"Why not?"

Dewey emailed back: "'I'm so glad things are working out. Thank you for your offer for' —what's that big word for payment that sounds like ruminating?—"

"Remuneration."

"Right. 'Thank you for your offer for re-nu-mer-ation. It's more of a hobby—' No, 'craft, of mine.' My payment is that we solved your problem!' There. That's good, right?"

"Right."

He sent it off.

"Phew," Dewey said as he plopped onto the couch. Maybe he'd watch something on their big screen, or take a nap. This had been quite a day. It had been quite a year.

Out of the corner of Dewey's eye, he saw Wolfie run over to the big lime green landing pillow. He greeted, not one, not two, not three, but four people, one bigger than the next, each shooting down the slide and tumbling into his office.

Pooh Bear, Stephanie, Mom, and Dad landed, each one on top of the next.

"See!" Pooh said. "What'd I tell you!"

Acknowledgments

Truth is, in a process like this one, there are lots of folks who were of great help. They were pulling for me, some without me knowing, because their own lives run so busy, fast, and full. I begin by thanking them. I suspect that their collective good wishes carried my little writing thoughts from dock out to sea. Thank you all for your good thoughts and wishing me well.

The writer's life is a bit like a heroic quest. So many of us experience what Joseph Campbell called "the refusal of the summons," as motherhood, fear of failure, fear of success, and a sense of inadequacy fill our heads instead of our pages. And then appears the magical helper who mentors us and says our quest can be done. For me, that person is CJ. Thank you for telling me to write. Again and again. Thank you to Jay Gordon for loving me enough to let me go, and still send me XOXOs and celebrate my successes on this journey.

To Dayna Anderson and all of Amberjack Publishing, who loved the concept of Dewey and brought it to others; my editor, Cherrita Lee, who cheers me on, encourages me, and helps me work through ideas; and my agent, Rebecca Angus, who not only represents me, but is an editor with a keen eye. I'm so fortunate to have the great artist, Agnieszka Grochalska, design my covers. That she brings my words to life from across the globe, where my husband's mother was born, has a lovely symmetry to it.

Stephanie Humphrey read my very first full Dewey draft and gave me feedback. I'm forever grateful for her time and care early in the process. Elinor was the first kid to ask to read my book, tucking Dewey among her clothes for her plane ride home. Katie let me use her real-life letter to her brother! Charlie, be nice! Joanna Van Trees and Julie Sisk have been true blue; Haleh Stahl offers such good advice; and my cousin, Vicki Winthrop, makes my heart sing and touches me day in and day out. Thank you to my husband, Bryan, for his never-ending love and support of me as well as my writing, and for being my partner in this journey called life. My son, Florian, inspires these books and inspires me. His very being has taught me that life does not always go as one plans, and therein lies magic. To Michael Ungar, who decided that this was the year to adopt us and finally made an honest daughter out of me. Thanks for being one of my biggest fans! Paula Rozomofsky, Horn Ungar, Elizabeth Sanders, Richard Friedman, Rela Cravens, the Winthrops, and the Horns—you have proven again and again that family shows up. Maybe that's why Dewey has such a good head on his shoulders. And when the going gets nuts, thanks to the Ks for making this problem-solving adventure more fun.

About the Author

Lorri Horn is the author of the Kirkus starred novel *Dewey Fairchild, Parent Problem Solver,* which was listed as one of the Best Middle-Grade Books of 2017 by Kirkus Reviews.

Lorri spent her childhood days in California and has been working with kids all her life. She got her first babysitting job when she was nine years old, became a camp counselor, and went on to be a teacher.

Fascinated by the origins of behavior, Lorri spent a few years studying *cercopithecus aethiops* (vervet monkeys) and thought she'd become a famous biological anthropologist. But it turns out there's a decent amount of camping involved in that career. Plus, while it was fascinating to study and observe our little non-human primate brothers and sisters, Lorri found it much more rewarding to share a good book with a kid. Not once did those vervets gather round for story-time.

So Lorri became an educator and an author for humans, who, admittedly, sometimes monkey around. She has a degree in English, a teaching credential, has been Nationally Board Certified, and has taught public school for over 14 years.

She loves cheese (if she had to choose between cheese and chocolate on a deserted island, she'd have to say cheese—and that's saying a whole lot, because she's not sure how'd she live without chocolate), humor, baking, books, and spending time with her husband, son, and their dog—you guessed it—Wolfie.